CARROLL & GRAF

Blue Harpsichord

Blue Harpsichord

Francis Steegmuller

Carroll & Graf Publishers, Inc.
New York

AMICO SCHAPIRO PRO MUSCIPULA GRATIAS

PART ONE

CHAPTER ONE

Terence Kelly, a rising young professor of Latin at the university, was inaugurating a new way of life for himself on this particular Wednesday in November, 1946 which happened to be his twenty-fifth birthday. It was known to himself as "the new program," and was a program of detachment. "Hands off! Hands off other people! Let them alone!" So it might be expressed, in brief.

It had been germinating for the past year or two, during which time Terence had been increasingly haunted by certain memories from his childhood, all of them reminding him of one thing: that in his case, somehow, the sharing of experience had always had a way of bringing on unfavorable consequences—unfavorable not only to himself but to the sharer as well.

Even in his boyhood there had been signs of this. Little signs, but signs nonetheless. If he volunteered to make a fire in the dining-room fireplace for his parents on a chilly morning—to take but one example—the fire was sure to smoke and drive everyone from the breakfast table. One nearly fatal day at a summer hotel, he showed off his skill on his new bicycle to his father by riding at low tide down a steep runway leading from a sea-wall to a floating dock; his emergency brake failed and he and the bicycle together flew into the mudflats. He almost suffocated, and his father, in extricating him, swallowed so much water and mud that he too was at death's door. At his first country-club dance, when he was fifteen, the music, the moonlight, the punch and the girls went to his head, and before he knew it he and his partner were being led off the floor for "improper dancing." They hadn't been dancing at all improperly—just gaily, with a pleasant abandon unusual in Terence's sober young life. It was one of the chaperons, vulgar and drunk, who rebuked and stopped them; but for a time, until a conference of parents and other chaperons straightened things out, both Terence and the nice little girl he'd been dancing with suffered agonies of adolescent humiliation.

There had been numerous such episodes. As he looked back on them now, Terence felt certain that they had played a far larger part in his life than he had previously realized. And because episodes like them had continued to plague him, he considered them the chief reason for the inauguration, at this late date, of "the new program."

He even wondered, at times, whether they were not perhaps the reason for his being in academic life. His father and grandfather had been lawyers, and in his early years he had supposed that he would be a lawyer too: how had he come to Latin-teaching, of all improbable professions? There had been no *decision*, either laborious or sudden, to go into it. He had seemed just to slip in, with his mother's approval. Why? Wasn't it perhaps a compensation for his distrust of himself in what most people took in their stride as casual, everyday relations with their fellows? Probably. And Latin had been a safe choice of subject. A Latin class wasn't something likely to affect the life of a modern student very deeply.

In any case, whatever had made him choose the academic profession, he was doing well in it. At his early age he had already left the rank of instructor behind him, and this very birthday was, as it turned out, being celebrated for him by the university, which had chosen it to inform him that his doctor's thesis was satisfactory and acceptable.

He was carrying his thesis with him that afternoon as he walked east on 57th Street, and he took it with him into a small millinery shop which he had often previously noticed in passing because of the presence in its window of a number of leather-bound books and a card saying that orders were taken for binding.

As he opened the door, which was inscribed "Helene-Chapeaux," he was greeted by a heavy smell of cooking, there was a rattle of pots and pans, and out from behind a pair of dirty portieres came an untidy, broken-down looking woman of middle age, wiping her hands on her dress. "Bonjour, Monsieur," she said, smiling overcordially. "Can I help you?"

Surprised and displeased—for from without the little shop had seemed rather chic—Terence pointed to the window and asked the cost of a certain style of binding.

"It all depends on ze size, Monsieur. A beeg book costs more zan a leetle wan. What size 'ave you?"

He opened his package and showed her the bulky type-written manuscript in its paper covers. The milliner made a gesture of dismay. "Mon dieu, Monsieur, qu'est-ce que c'est que ça?"

"It's a thesis. I'd like . . ."

"A teesis?"

"A thesis. Ma thèse d'université, Madame."

But the French seemed not to help her, and she put a hand on his arm. "Leave the book here, Monsieur," she urged, "and I will talk to ze gentleman who does my work. Come back tomorrow and I will have ze information."

But Terence shook his head. This woman was too squalid to have dealings with; she smiled at him too familiarly, putting her face too close to his. And the bindings in the window, he now saw, although they seemed of good workmanship, were flyspecked and faded. There was a dismal and depressing air about the place.

"Leave it, Monsieur. It will be quite safe."

"I tell you what I'll do," he said, to get away. "I pass by here quite often. I'll stop in again and talk to the gentleman myself. I suppose he comes here? What's the best time?"

She leaned toward him and this time smiled almost conspiratorially. "At night, Monsieur. Come tonight and you'll see him—me rid-hidded Oirish by-frind. And bring in ze girlfren' sometime, and buy her a nice leetle 'at."

Terence glanced at her sharply. Surely in the word *hat*, her word of words, a French milliner in New York would have learned to pronounce an *h* if she could pronounce one at all. And this woman could. She had pronounced several. What was she, anyway, with her weird mish-mash of accents?

As she mentioned his girl friend she gave a crazy leer and Terence hastily bade her good-bye and walked out, breathing deeply and gratefully of the fresh air. Having been within the shop, he now marveled, glancing at its exterior with new eyes, that he should ever have entered it.

He dropped the card, "Helene-Chapeaux," into the gutter as he walked on toward Sutton Place.

CHAPTER TWO

Cynthia, Iris and Liz—The Three, as they called themselves—were waiting for him, ready for their Latin lesson.

It was uncharacteristic of them to be ready on time. Usually the two at whose flats the lesson was not being given that week strolled in anywhere up to half an hour late, and sometimes even the hostess herself wasn't on hand when she should be. Always the lesson was punctuated by lengthy, non-scholarly digressions on the part of the students. Terence, regular and precise himself, had found all this annoying at first. But he had rapidly come to realize that The Three were in every way rather distantly removed from any acquaintances he had ever had in the past, and that their standards might well be suited to the lives they led. He told them coolly one day that he had decided to charge them double for all time not actually spent at work on Latin, and they had hilariously approved. This new fee schedule was bringing him in quite a pleasant income from The Three.

His conscience hurt him about only one of them. Not about Cynthia, the present Mrs. Zug, whose far from threadbare apartment on the East River was school to-day: *she* could afford any charges he chose to make. And so could Liz, Contessa di Cesare, who had been the first Mrs. Zug and now lived with the Conte not far away, in surroundings equally eloquent of comfort. But Iris, the middle one . . .

Poor Iris Penn-Gillis! Her husband had recently been in Reno, and—so the others had told Terence one day when she'd played hookey—toward him she'd acted so nobly that her friends thought her mad. To refuse to take alimony from a Penn-Gillis because you still loved him! Did that make sense? Scarcely, to anyone whose head was screwed on properly. But that was Iris for you. Idealistic. Her own worst enemy. As yet she'd made no definite arrangements about her future, and was scrimping along temporarily in furnished rooms on the West Side. The West Side! That thought depressed the other two immeasurably. They'd all lived there at one time or another, of course, during their somewhat variegated pasts, but to think that Iris was *back* there! The entire Penn-Gillis clan was probably laughing their heads off at her. How glad they'd been to get rid of her, the dirty snobs. Glad enough to be willing to pay plenty. And Iris had taken nothing. Nothing, poor crazy girl.

Yes—poor Iris. Could she afford to pay double for Terence's wasted hours? Probably not. Terence planned to make a special financial arrangement with her when he could speak with her privately. God, how beautiful she was! Even more beautiful than the others.

At first all The Three had struck Terence as being so alike as to be almost indistinguishable: equally beautiful, equally perfectly got together, equally devoid of individual characteristics. And then gradually Iris had begun to emerge. Why? Because she was really the most beautiful? Or possibly because she was the only one, at the moment, who was unattached?

The others had gradually emerged a little, too. A very little. Liz seemed the bubbliest, perhaps; Cynthia the bossiest.

"Good afternoon, Professor!" They greeted him mockingly as he came in.

"*Carinissimo professore!*" cried Liz. She hadn't been married to the Conte more than a few years, but he'd

14

had a marked effect on her speech from the moment of their engagement. "*Carino istitutore!*"

None of The Three had ever studied a dead language before, and Terence gathered that there was something fantastic and fascinating to them in the idea. Each week they seemed to embark on their lesson as though they were undertaking something uncanny and thrilling—almost like risking an encounter with death itself.

There was considerable rivalry at the university for the downtown tutoring jobs—those plums that are prominent among the advantages which city institutions of learning can offer their faculty members. There was no particular reason why Terence, rather than someone else in the department, should have got the job with The Three, except that he luckily happened to be in the office of the department chairman just when Cynthia's telephone call was routed through by the university switchboard. "A clean-cut American boy!" Liz sighed, when Terence had left Cynthia's flat after the highly satisfactory preliminary interview. "*Giovane americanissimo igienico.* Just the thing—don't you agree?" The others did.

"Good afternoon, ladies," Terence greeted them today. "*Salve!* Shall we open to page twenty? I think you'll all enjoy the Ablative Absolute. Everybody does. Nothing tricky about it, nothing involved. Now then . . ."

Terence's manner was always more breezy in the classroom than elsewhere.

The Three were breezy everywhere.

"Oh, Terence!"

"Yes, Liz?" (It had become an informal kind of class after the first lesson or two.)

"Girls can't concentrate with packages around. You ought to learn that, Terence. What's in it? Something for us?"

"No, nothing for you. Just my thesis. I almost left it to be bound today, and then didn't."

"Your thesis!"

"His thesis!"

"Oo, let's all *look!*"

"Terry darling, all my *life* I've wondered what a thesis looks like. . . ."

"*Carinissimo professore . . .*"

They all crowded around.

And later, at the end of the lesson, when he let them know that it was his birthday, glad cries rang out again.

"Hap-pay birth-day tooo yoooo. . . ."

"*Quanti anni hai, caro Terenzio?*"

"*Troppi .*"

"*Non credo. Bambino! Ragazzino!*"

Cynthia had the butler bring in champagne and started to call up friends and make it a party, but Terence stopped her—he'd have to be leaving before anybody could get there. "Here's a toast to you, Terence," she said. "Is there anything special about you we should drink to?"

"Well, if you'd like to drink to the new program . . ."

"The new program!"

"What's that, Terence?"

"Come clean, Professor!"

But Terence just smiled.

"To the new program, then," said Cynthia, "whatever the hell it is."

Terence didn't have the heart to charge double for the lengthier than usual non-Latin part of this particular afternoon. Otherwise it was a fairly typical lesson.

Mr. Zug, a large, sleek, immensely prosperous-looking man, came in from the Street before Terence left. He was overjoyed to find The Three. He loved their congeniality: it flattered him every time he thought of it.

"We get together so much less often than we used to," he lamented, kissing them enthusiastically in inverse order. "It's a ———————ing shame, if you ask me."

"The Opera will remedy that," said Cynthia. "Next Monday night's the opening. Remember, Terence, we're counting on you. Next Monday night. And then every once in a while all winter long."

Zug had done a big favor on the Street for one of the Opera House people recently, and the use of a box from time to time had been gratefully offered in return and accepted with enthusiasm.

Terence thought that Zug was looking at him a little queerly. He had to leave then, and Iris said she'd leave with him. They said good-bye to the others in the drawing room. "A *professor?*" Terence heard Zug say, as the butler was letting them out. "A *professor* we're going in for now? Where's the fun? What's the idea?"

Cynthia waited till she heard the door close. "Now Zugie—you know all about that. The professor and Iris—we've been all over it. You know we have."

"Oh yes, yes. So we have. . . ."

"Such a *nice* professor," Liz said reassuringly. "Such a nice, clean-cut, American type of boy. . . ."

Out on the street, Iris said she had the blues and felt like walking part of the way, if Terence had the time. He didn't but said he did, and in the twilight they strolled westward, heads of passersby turning in admiration as they always did when Iris strolled. In the distance a sunset glow lingered in the November sky, broken into here and there by the silhouettes of New York's towers.

Terence wondered about Iris. Could he aspire to her? Not only was she outside his sphere, but also, he knew, her thoughts were still with Penn-Gillis. She had left Zug for him, and then purely because of family pressure he'd ditched her after the briefest of married lives. She was sad, sad. This *might* be the perfect time to urge himself on her attention. In a purely consolatory way, of course. On a frankly lower plane. Was there a chance of success? Terence didn't know. He couldn't decide. He wished he could be surer: her very devotion to someone else made her ideal for his purpose.

"Life's delicious," Iris was saying, savagely. "Delicious, isn't it? Like hell it is. Like bloody hell." She had a somber, brooding look. "You think you're all set at last, and then smacko . . ."

Terence decided that this would not be a good moment. He murmured something sympathetic. Then he noticed that they were passing the millinery shop with books in the window, and through the glass he saw Helene herself, smiling her unattractive smile at the hatted reflection of a customer in the dressing-table mirror. He stood still as he suddenly remembered. "Damn it —I've gone and left my thesis at Cynthia's."

"Oh, let's go back for it. We'll pick it up, then take a taxi."

But Terence, glancing at his watch, shook his head. He'd be late enough as it was. He'd have to take a taxi right now, at least as far as the subway. That was the trouble with leading two (or more) different kinds of lives in New York. The various settings were apt to be so far apart, physically as well as otherwise. In such unrelated quarters of town. One spent so much time traveling. As to the thesis, he was in no immediate need of it. He'd pick it up the next time he went to Cynthia's, or Cynthia could bring it to the next Latin class. It was of no importance.

He hailed a taxi and they climbed in.

"Don't bother about me if you're rushed," said Iris, as nicely as though she weren't beautiful at all. "Just drop me anywhere—at whatever corner's the most convenient."

But Terence took her to her door. They said goodbye. Then suddenly he could scarcely believe his ears. "Won't you make a habit of me?" Iris was asking, looking at him disturbingly. "I'd like that. You know I'm not happy this year. But I like you."

Her voice was so humble! Terence could manage only a gulp and a handclasp; and then she was gone, smiling back at him as she disappeared He rode uptown in a glow. A habit of her! A habit of Iris. . . .

CHAPTER THREE

He was late for dinner at Ramsay's.

Ramsay scolded him. "The hot canapés are *stiff* with cold," he said. "Where have you *been?*"

Ramsay had a lilting way of talking. A manner of enunciation that had caused generations of undergraduates to call him Ramsay Pamsay and that had helped make it impossible for the university to respect him. At fifty he was still an instructor in the art department: never a promotion since joining the faculty twenty-five years before! But the university had never forced him out, as it forced out most unpromotables: it seemed to think that there was room on the campus for one Ramsay, as long as he didn't cost too much.

After all, teaching still counted for something—just a little—and Ramsay was always appreciated by some of his students. A few. Usually the more dilettantish ones, or at least those who, even if they were perforce going in for serious careers of one kind or another, had a yearning toward dilettantism. Not that Ramsay was a dilettante himself. Nothing could be more meticulous than his little productions. But they were indeed little. Not nearly as long and weighty as most of the faculty publications, which were accorded very considerable importance indeed by their authors and by the university itself. Theses, many of them: Ramsay's great sin in the university's eyes was that he had never bothered to write one. He hadn't wanted to, and he hadn't done it: he had refused to conform, as almost everyone else, including Terence, had conformed. Instead, he pleased himself, and wrote what he called his "detective stories," his "mysteries."

Ramsay poured Terence sherry, passed him the stiffened canapés, and showed him the material for his current mystery. It consisted of a series of three photographs—photographs of a fifteenth-century triptych, acquired just a few days before by the art museum downtown after having been discovered by one of the museum's scouts in an unlikely place—a chapel on one of the Dutch West Indian islands. Ramsay was always one of the first to be called in to look at the museum's newly acquired paintings, and he was always given photographs of any that interested him. This one was undoubtedly Flemish, he said, but it was unsigned and unidentified. "Look carefully," he said. "See if you can find what's mysterious."

Terence looked. Scenes from the life of the Holy Family. No, not quite. Scenes from the life of Saint Joseph, rather. Joseph was the principal character in each of the panels. Mary was present only in the second two, Jesus only in the third. But what was mysterious about it? The first panel clearly showed Saint Joseph as a youth. Then the marriage of Joseph and Mary, and then the Holy Family. Underneath the central panel, in a horizontal supplementary scene, was the death of Joseph. Everything seemed clear enough. Terence could find no mystery.

Ramsay laughed. "Don't you see? Don't you see that . . ."

But the smell of something burning came from the kitchen, and Ramsay had to run. There was never a cook at Ramsay's—there wasn't enough money for more than a cleaning woman occasionally.

"Haven't you found it yet?" he demanded, when he came back. "Look. In each of the panels Joseph is portrayed as a carpenter, with his carpenter's bench beside him. Don't you notice something missing from the bench in the supplementary panel? Something that's present in the three main ones?"

Terence peered, and peered again. "The mousetrap! It's gone!"

"Completely gone. Absolutely vanished off the bench. Why? What *is* the mousetrap anyway? And why should it disappear? There's an answer to each of those questions, if I can only find it. Those old painters had a reason for everything they did."

Ramsay's "detective stories" were rather celebrated in academic art circles. Every once in a while one of them was printed, with illustrations, in some scholarly periodical. Why did the same, unidentifiable church steeple appear in so many early English religious paintings by different painters? Why did every portrait bust found in every tomb at El-Azoum on the Nile lack the lobe of the left ear? Why indeed? Ramsay was known for his ingenious, scholarly answers.

His mother had long lived with him until her death a few years before; now he lived alone in the little apartment, apparently untroubled by the university's lack of esteem; he taught his small classes and haunted the library stacks, gathering material for his mysteries. That was his life. He seldom went downtown, or to anybody's house. He was a university monk if ever there was one. Terence had admired him since attending one of his seminars. These days he didn't see Ramsay as much as he would have liked to: in a university, just as everywhere else, one is apt to lose sight of old friends when a career's in the making.

Ramsay began to bring food out of the kitchen, and when everything was ready and they were about to sit down, he poured more sherry and raised his glass. There was no jealousy in Ramsay, no question of his holding one's career or one's youth against one. He was a kindly old monk. "To your thesis!" he said. "And happy birthday!"

Terence thanked him. They made quite a contrast as they stood there: Ramsay thin, stooped, shabby and spectacled; and Terence with the appearance of a well-dressed, prosperous young business man. And Terence was conscious of how contrasting their situations were, as well. But he preferred Ramsay's company to that of most of the other ambitious young members of the faculty like himself.

In addition to his teaching and his non-comformity, Terence admired and valued another of Ramsay's qualities: his detachment. Discussion of personal affairs was something he didn't indulge in: he gave the impression of having none himself, and assuming that no one else had any either. If one talked about one's self in his presence he simply sat there politely until the subject seemed to be exhausted. At such times he never dreamed of expressing an opinion: it was impossible to imagine Ramsay giving advice or interfering.

For this very reason Terence, elsewhere so reserved,

was apt at Ramsay's to indulge in the rare catharsis of talking rather freely about himself. Tonight was no exception, and he found himself reminiscing—about Paris, chiefly.

He had always lived at home, even during and after college. And then he had been in uniform almost three years, overseas almost two, a lieutenant in one of the Paris military offices. "Don't send me any cables, Terence," his mother had ordered him before he left. "I'll be afraid of telegrams till the war's over." Of course he had done as she asked: Terence had always tended to do whatever his mother ordered, whether it was to "Stand up straight, Terence," or "Remember you're a gentleman, Terence," or "Keep your hands off the girls, Terence," which was the one she'd uttered most frequently as he'd put his boyhood behind him. Mrs. Kelly had been a great utterer of injunctions: she had had to be, she was accustomed to explain to everyone, since her husband had not lived to provide his son with a father's guidance.

Being in Paris, it occurred to him to have a French dress made for his mother. She sent him her measurements, and he took them to a well-known establishment and chose a style and material. "Ah, monsieur," the saleswoman said when he stopped in to see how it was coming along. "I am glad you have come. It is difficult to make a dress merely with measurements—without a model. We have been lucky to find in the workroom a young person who seems to have almost the exact measurements of *madame votre mère*, and we have proceeded to make the dress on her. I was hoping that you would stop by, so that you could look at her yourself, to see whether we are not right."

Terence stared with interest at the blushing girl who

emerged from the rear of the premises and whose measurements were pointed out by the saleswoman as being "uncannily like those of *madame votre mère*." Not being a model by profession, the saleswoman explained, the girl was unaccustomed to the scrutiny of customers. "You have the present sad state of France to thank for this fortunate coincidence, Monsieur," she said. "In ordinary times Mademoiselle Madeleine would be plump, but with food rations as they are she is *mince comme une femme chic américaine de n'importe quelle age.*"

Terence remembered that a week or so later when Mademoiselle Madeleine herself delivered the dress to him at his hotel late one afternoon, and he offered her a handful of candy and other PX delicacies that made her blush again, this time from pleasure. "Monsieur," she said, "I was not going to do something that I was told to do, but you are so kind that I will. I was told to try on the dress for you, to show you how it will look on *madame votre mère*." She changed into it while he turned politely away, and they discussed it, she examining it and herself in the long mirror of Terence's armoire. She pointed out several improvements that might be made, and then, since it was time for her to take the dress off, waited for him to turn away again. He didn't turn, but she took off the dress eventually anyway.

They were often together during the next few weeks. It was a simple affair, as Madeleine was a simple girl, but there was nothing simple about the new world of feelings she made Terence aware of. He was gay and relaxed as never before in his life.

When she met him the afternoon of V-E Day, she brought with her the dress, finally made right, and that evening she wore it when they went to dinner in a noisy restaurant and later joined the dancing crowds in the streets. In the midst of their celebrations he sent his mother, to whom he had lately been writing less regularly than usual, a happy cable of affection and end-of-the-war sentiments. Two days later he had a cable in return—from his aunt, bearing the news of his mother's death. And soon came a letter, also from his aunt, which carefully didn't blame him, but let him know that the sight of the yellow envelope, even though the war was over, had been the immediate cause.

He learned afterward from his mother's doctor what had hitherto been kept from him—that for some time her heart had been in such state that any surprise could have had the same effect. But the episode shook him. Relations with Madeleine ended abruptly. She was a sentimental member of the extremely petite bourgeoisie, and she assured Terence that she understood his decision perfectly. She admired it as a true act of mourning, she said, and she wept all the harder at fate for separating her from one whose feelings were characterized by such *délicatesse*. Terence gave her the dress.

On one of the rare evenings he hadn't spent with Madeleine, he had gone with officer acquaintances to a USO concert at the Olympia—an enjoyable occasion at which a pretty young American harpsichordist named Myra Drysdale played everything from Bach to Basin Street on her versatile instrument, much to the joy of the uniformed audience. One of Terence's party, a musician, filled with enthusiasm and claiming to be "a good friend of Myra's," took them all backstage; and although Myra was clearly unable to place her "good friend" she was friendly and pleasant with everyone. There was a quality about her that made itself felt at once—something sympathetic and outgoing that doubtless went far toward explaining the attractiveness of her concert. Terence remembered this later, following the episode of the fatal cable, and at the end of another of her concerts he found himself, in his loneliness, going backstage again, waiting till her other visitors had left, and asking her if she wouldn't come with him to the club in the Crillon. By the time her tour took her away from Paris they had become fast friends.

With Myra, Terence found himself able to speak of many things. They discussed the feeling of guilt he couldn't shake off—guilt at the result of the message so carelessly sent his mother while celebrating with "French friends," as he always put it. Myra, who was almost exactly his age, tried so hard and kindly to make him see his innocence in the matter that he pretended to be more convinced than he was. In her presence he felt so much better than out of it that several times before she left he almost asked her to marry him. But something held him back. And although he had seen her constantly since they had both returned to New York, and had never ceased for a moment to appreciate her, even to appreciate her increasingly, something had always still held him back.

He often wondered what this reluctance was—as he knew Myra had been wondering for some time too. She had lately shown unmistakeable signs of dissatisfaction with the role she had been filling for so long. And his wondering had seemed to bring out from their hiding place in the back of his mind those memories of disastrous shared experiences in early life—those memories that had led him, a few weeks before, to move out of his aunt's rooming house, where Myra lived, and that had now caused him to inaugurate definitively "the new program."

Hands off! Hands off other people! Let them alone! To follow such precepts completely, of course, one would have to be a Ramsay—a condition impossible for most people to fulfill even if they wanted to. And yet for him Ramsay's direction, at least, was the proper one.

Yes, he was cut out as definitely for one kind of bachelorhood as Ramsay was for another. Myra's name wasn't written on any page of the new program. It was for her own good as well as his that it wasn't. But even Terence knew better than to try to explain such things to a girl. So of late he had been saying less and less to Myra about anything at all.

Terence suppressed several smiles during the course of these birthday reminiscences. Ramsay was being so kind, so polite. Not only pouring him brandy, but even remembering to nod occasionally, as though he were really listening, really interested. Whereas Terence knew quite well that his thoughts were miles away—with St. Joseph and the missing mousetrap, probably, or in some similar company.

"I'd better go, Ramsay," he said, finally, when it grew late. "Thanks a lot for letting me listen to myself as a birthday present."

Polite to the end, Ramsay hastily returned from whatever world he had been living in. "Goodness—don't leave on my account, dear boy. Talk as long as you like. . . ."

But Terence said good-night.

As he walked the short distance to the campus, he made the nightly examination of conscience that had become his habit. Had he, during the day, done anything that might have the kind of consequences he dreaded? In the morning, acceptance of his thesis; and just before and after lunch, his regular Latin classes: nothing startling there. In the afternoon The Three. Terence smiled to himself: certainly The Three were safely detached and remote! Even Iris, or, looking at it another way, especially Iris. A bachelor, plagued by demands that were all the stronger as the result of memories of Paris, demands that made one know one couldn't be a Ramsay, needed someone. And Iris seemed ideal: available, and yet infatuated with her husband, or rather her ex-husband, and thus holding out the prospect of pleasure without entanglement. . . .

All day, too, he had carefully avoided his Aunt Kitty, who would have poured heaven knew what birthday sentimentalities over his head and reproached him for his treatment of both her and Myra. And he had declined Myra's suggestion that they spend the evening together, and had deliberately gone to safe, admirable old Ramsay instead.

That was all, wasn't it? A safe day—another safe one, thank God. A day calculated to further the aims of the program that it initiated. Oh yes—there had been one more episode, if one wanted to record every last detail: the visit to the milliner. But even Terence wasn't morbid about mere shopping encounters.

CHAPTER FOUR

Red usually stopped off at the Hibernia Bar and Grille on his way to Helene's. "Just having a couple of shots on Second Avenue," he answered her if she asked him what he'd been doing. "Why, what's it to you?"

So she seldom asked. Tonight he'd have been lying if he'd said "a couple of shots": he was late, and there were clearly a good many more shots than that inside him. Helene felt apprehensive. Red was capable of overdoing things after stopping on Second Avenue too long.

He was a big, handsome fellow: so Helene thought him, anyway. Twice as big as she was, and dirty in the evening after his day in the park. He was selling balloons at present, the book-binding business—his, at least,—being what it was.

"Somebody come in today, Red," Helene called to him in the bathroom, where he was washing up. She thought the news might sweeten him, neutralize the extra drinks. "Some fella come in about a binding. Said he'd come back."

"Come back?" Red emerged, wiping himself with a bath towel. His blue eyes had an especially piercing look that Helene knew well enough to dislike. And he spoke in a special, quiet voice that she had equal reason not to care for. "Come back when?" There was a hint of a brogue in Red's voice, especially when he spoke in this careful, quiet way.

"Some time tonight, he said."

"Why didn't you keep him here, so I could see him?"

"How could I, Red? He come in around four. How could I hold him till now?"

"So what'd you do? Send him to your other gentleman friend?"

"Oh, Red. . . ." Helene had had book-binding relations with someone else before Red had entered her life, and it was quite impossible to convince him of the truth—that the earlier arrangement had been a purely business one.

"You didn't send him to your other gentleman friend?" Red asked, coming over to her. "You're sure?" He took one of her arms in his big hands and gave it a little twist. "Sure, sweetheart?"

Helene trembled. "Don't, Red," she begged. "Don't start being mean just because some little jerk come in.

Really I didn't send him anywhere else. You know I wouldn't. He just come and went. Really."

Red smiled at her and went over to the closet where the bottle was. The bottle! That was the last thing Helene liked to see him go for at any time. But especially tonight, with that look in his eye. She kept trembling with various kinds of anticipation as she got their supper ready. She could never tell, of course. Sometimes things turned out to be just as wonderful as she'd expected them to be horrible. It was never possible to know in advance, with Red. A black eye, or ecstasy, or sometimes a combination of both. . . . That was Red's charm—for Helene.

CHAPTER FIVE

Terence's Aunt Kitty Quinn did so wish that he might have spent his birthday evening with her, or at least come to see her during the day. She was seriously displeased that he had done neither. Chiefly because she missed his affection. But also because there was something she had particularly wanted to talk over with him.

Gus Lefferts was legally dead today. He had been absent, silent and untraceable, the necessary seven years, and now the court order had come. Just today. Now she could consider as her own the few thousand dollars he had left in his bank. Now, if she wished, which she didn't, and if she were given an opportunity, than which nothing seemed more unlikely, she could marry again. Marry *again*, that is, in the eyes of the law. For only in the eyes of the law—not in her own eyes—had she been married the first time.

Poor Gus! Where could he be? Not for a minute did Miss Quinn believe that he was really dead. He had just disappeared, like the sweet fellow he was. He must have taken considerable trouble to do it so thoroughly. How grateful she was to him! A true nature's gentleman if there ever was one. And a fine figure of a man as well. A little fleshy, perhaps, for some people's tastes. But not for hers, nor for his own. That had been one of the first subjects he'd mentioned, at the very beginning of the whirlwind Atlantic City courtship. "You're a skinny little thing, aren't you," he said, appraisingly, almost the minute they'd started talking at the pickle-bar, that first afternoon of her vacation. "How do you know you're there when you wake up in the morning?"

Miss Quinn hadn't known quite how to answer that: it wasn't a question she could remember having been asked before.

"Now me," he went on, with a smile that went all the way across his big round face, "the minute I wake up I can feel myself all there in a big way under the sheets. It's comfortable, sorta. Wouldn't you like to be comfortable with me, honey?"

And then and there Miss Quinn felt something melt inside her, and she knew that an offer of comfort with this jolly fellow was, especially for someone of her age, like an offer of the grace of God. There was no question of declining it. The only difference was, as it turned out, that she had to compromise to get it and that in the end it eluded her anyway.

They talked a little longer, and met again that evening on the boardwalk, after Gus had closed the pickle-bar for the night. The company was promoting him, it seemed. They were taking him away from the bar and putting him on the road—he'd be a real traveling sales-man, with a car and a territory. A territory in the middle west somewhere. But the home office was in New York, and he'd be there regularly, and he wanted a home nearby. "You'll keep house for me, won't you?" he asked. "You'd be the sweetest little housekeeper a fellow could have."

And then it turned out that he'd never been bap-tized, and never would be. So there could be no ques-tion of marriage. "Marriage without baptism is a mock-ery in my eyes," said Miss Quinn. "Why don't you just *get* baptized? In any church—I won't hold you to mine. Baptism's nothing to be afraid of. It's nothing but a few drops of holy water."

But Gus shook his head, and looked as grim as it was possible for him to look: you could see that he really was, as he put it, "allergic to religion."

Miss Quinn was sure that that was a state which wouldn't last too long if Gus had the heart she felt he had. So sure that she summoned up all her courage and whispered that she wouldn't mind not being married for the time being, if he understood what she meant. He understood it, but he wouldn't hear of it. "A nice little thing like you?" he said. "It wouldn't be right. I wouldn't take the responsibility. Besides, this is a big event in *my* life. I want to be respectable for a change. So we'll just go to the City Hall. . . ."

She patiently explained why they wouldn't. Marriage to a non-baptized person was impossible. Marriage to a baptized non-Catholic was solemnized by a priest in a rectory. Civil ceremonies were not recognized. Gus looked baffled, but patted her hand and smiled cheer-fully. "We'll figure something out, Sugar. . . ."

The next day he didn't work, and they went out on a fishing boat with some other vacationists. She didn't fish, and couldn't think—just sat around feeling miserable as the boat rolled, and wondering what was going to happen to her in the next minute or two. After lunch (not that *she* could eat any of it!) Gus took her hand and looked at her in a way that she sensed meant something. "We're beyond the three-mile limit, Sugar."

"We are?"

"Look what I bought this morning." She looked. A plain gold band. "We'll have it marked inside later."

"Will we?"

"Yes. I've been talking to the captain, Kitty. He'll marry us. Of course we'll have to do it quick, before we get back closer to shore. So what do you say?"

"Oh, Gus, I told you. . . ."

"I know: it doesn't mean anything to you. But it won't harm you. And it means a hell of a lot to me, honey."

What could she do? Feeling as she did, especially. If ignorance was ever invincible it was Gus's. The captain married them in the cabin, with two of his crew as witnesses, while everybody else was too busy fishing to know what was going on.

In many ways she was wonderfully happy in the little apartment in Yonkers—happier than she'd ever been before or since. With a man like Gus around the house, contentedly smoking his pipe, playing his flute, reading his weekly *Pickle Gazette* or a book of philosophy, who wouldn't be happy? Even if the book was usually a treatise by Robert Ingersoll, or a tale by Voltaire, or some other such atheistical rubbish.

She never told anyone she was married, because she never considered herself so. It was hard on her: even her closest sister, Terence's mother, refused to visit her at the little apartment in Yonkers because she naturally thought Kitty and Gus were living in sin—as indeed, in a sense, they were. Terence himself, her darling nephew, was allowed to see her only rarely. She couldn't go to confession. And hardest of all was the fact that Gus's heart, so soft in other ways, never softened as she'd hoped it would.

"Gus?"

"Yes, Sugar?"

"Remember you told me that even if having the captain marry us didn't mean anything to me it wouldn't harm me?"

"Yes—well?"

"Well, that's what I think about baptism and you."

Silence.

"Won't you please come with me to a priest?"

Silence.

"Or to *somebody*?"

Silence.

"Won't you?"

"Now Kitty, don't let's . . ."

Despite the happy parts, it became intolerable after a year or so. Intolerable to be properly married according to other people's ideas and yet unable to say she was married at all, because according to her own ideas she wasn't. Intolerable to brood on Gus's selfishness: surely he'd do that one little thing for her if he really loved her! And intolerable to hear herself nagging him about it. She hated herself for irritating so good and good-natured a man, destroying his comfort and her own. Not once did he lose his temper with her. But she knew, before the end, that he wouldn't put up with it much longer. Why should he?

The day she found the note on the bureau, lying there with the bankbook, she was scarcely surprised. "So long for good, Kitty. We could have been happy." She didn't blame him, even when she was sobbing the loudest. She went to confession, received absolution, and followed the priest's advice about reporting Gus's disappearance to the police. There was never a trace. He'd disappeared, his company said—vanished: of course she knew they were protecting him. How clear it was that he never wanted to see her or hear from her again! A lovely man, whom the inexorable twin forces of invincible ignorance and heavenly law had tragically kept her from making her own.

The money she never touched. It was in both their names, or rather in his name and the name of Kitty Lefferts, and she didn't feel herself entitled to it. She moved into Manhattan, rented a house and took roomers.

But now, beginning today, her feeling about the money was different. It was as though Gus, in legally dying, had left it to her. Why shouldn't she accept it? People accepted legacies from people whom they'd never met, or met but once; surely she could accept his. He would want her to.

It wasn't the acceptance of the money, but a certain use for it, that she had wanted to talk over with Terence. But more than anything else she had wanted him just to be with her for at least part of his birthday. His twenty-fifth birthday, especially. As aunts do, Miss Quinn thought most naturally of her nephew as the schoolboy she'd treated to Saturday lunches when his mother had allowed it, and given a new five-dollar bill to at Christmas. Even after he was twenty-one and out of college and in the army it was hard for her to remember that he'd become a man. But a twenty-fifth birthday: that made even her aware that now he was adult. An educated man; as educated as his father had been, though along different lines; a man to be consulted. But he "couldn't," he said, be with her for even half an hour on his birthday. "Couldn't!" His only relation in New York—the aunt of his childhood! Whoever it was that he chose to be with, though no doubt more educated and like himself than she now was, couldn't have the qualifications she had as *birthday* company. Not to speak of poor Myra. . . .

Miss Quinn was hurt. Hurt and affronted to the point of defiance: spirit wasn't a quality she had ever lacked. Terence had always been a sweet boy, as considerate a nephew as any aunt could ask for. Miss Quinn wished he might have remained so, but she had no intention of supplicating him. If he wouldn't come and see her on his birthday, why should she do him the honor of consulting him? She was still capable of managing her own affairs, wasn't she? The advice of an educated nephew was, after all, a luxury—and she'd never been dependent on luxuries in her life.

So it was without first asking Terence's opinion that Miss Quinn copied out, that evening, the draft of a letter she had prepared.

"Dear Reverend Mother: Since receiving your kind reply to my letter of inquiry, I have definitely decided that I wish in the near future to retire from active business and pass my remaining years in your Home. Mount St. Margaret's looks beautiful from the photographs. I enclose your application blank which I have filled out. You will notice that although I have several living relatives I am quite independent and answerable to no one but myself in financial affairs. . . ."

When it was done she walked out and mailed it at the corner.

CHAPTER SIX

As though Terence's behavior weren't trouble enough for a girl to be having, Myra Drysdale was close to desperation about her harpsichord. It seemed to be bringing her nothing but bad luck. Good luck mixed with a little bad was what one liked to consider normal. Bad luck mixed with a little good really *was* normal—or at least it seemed to be, in a musician's life. But bad luck alone, pure and unadulterated . . .

Should she abandon the harpsichord? Change instruments, so to speak, in mid-career? She had already done that once, in a sense. Now should she do it again? Now that the harpsichord was finally paid for? She'd lose money if she sold it—one always lost money on such occasions. But it was beginning to look as if even that might prove to be less expensive in the end than keeping the thing around.

The record company had been so polite. "Could we use your harpsichord, Miss Drysdale? We know you have such a wonderful one. We want a little background music for some eighteenth-century songs we're recording. We'd love to ask you to play it for us, but we're afraid we can't afford so fine an artist for this project. We'll just use one of our studio people. We'll pay the cartage both ways and fifty dollars rental. We wouldn't keep it more than two days."

Fifty dollars happened to be just the amount of the last installment due on the harpsichord. Besides, it was well to be nice to a record company if you hoped to be asked to make records some day. "Call my agent," Myra said. "Max Kramer. If it's OK with him it is with me."

The record company called back shortly to say that Max had given his approval, and the harpsichord was picked up and returned and the fifty dollars paid. It was a few months afterward—just today—that Myra learned what it had really been used for. The record company did indeed issue a set of eighteenth-century songs. But they weren't sung. They were played on the harpsichord—Myra's harpsichord—by Lily White, the other harpsichordist. And the record reviewers were already praising the beautiful tone of Lily's instrument. . . .

"What kind of an agent are you, Max?" Myra demanded, after she'd temporarily stopped crying. "*Whose* agent are you—Lily's or mine? Now the market for harpsichord records is glutted—you know what a small demand there is. Now I shan't be asked to make any records for years, if ever. And Lily gets this wonderful boost."

"True," said Max, mournfully. "True, Myra. My fault. My mistake."

If that wasn't like an agent!

"But you don't help to me, Myra," Max quickly added, in an accusing voice and in language that was as close to English as he usually came. "For this cut-skin game of concerts and contracts you're too nice. Knowing you're so nice makes it hard for me to be hard-boiled on your respect. It's your fault yet, Myra. If only you'd help to me by not always being so nice yourself already. . . ."

Myra gritted her teeth. She *was* nice, but she didn't like to be told so. "If I'm nice then it's up to you to be all the nastier," she said, crossly. "That's what you get twenty percent for, isn't it? To be nasty so I don't have to?" Then she began to cry again and hung up, and didn't answer the phone when it rang right away because she knew it would only be Max, calling her back in distress to say something else well-meant but unhelpful.

Most musicians' agents probably made too many mistakes, she supposed, from their clients' point of view. But only Max, so far as she knew, had ever let a rival harpsichordist make a name for herself on his client's harpsichord. On the other hand, she had to be fair to him: it was Max who had suggested the harpsichord in the first place. He'd heard Myra play the piano at a party one night, and had come over and introduced himself and said she had a real "harpsichordic touch." "Why don't you try it?" he asked. "I predict you a quick success. Much quicker than if you continue—excuse me—to be just one of the million good pianists in New York."

So she'd tried it, and it had been fun to play in the little night-clubs where Max had quickly got her engagements. "New Orleans and Chicago on the harpsichord": it was a novelty that everybody seemed to like. And then the USO tour, with her harpsichord traveling thousands of miles with her in airplanes and resounding in all kinds of unlikely places. But after she'd got back the bad luck had begun. One night-club cancellation after another due to bad business and a series of freakish circumstances, and now this absurd incident with the record company.

Myra had her living to earn, and of late she certainly hadn't been earning it very well. It was a question of having faith in the harpsichord and in Max. Should she have it? It was more profitable to play in night-clubs than to give piano lessons, and night-club work left her more time for practice on both instruments. But her money was running short. And Max seemed to have no suggestions to offer.

What was the best thing to do? Sell the harpsichord,

and trust that some piano pupils would turn up? Or keep hoping a little longer for an engagement? How she wished she could talk it over with Terence! But talks with Terence were pretty clearly a thing of the past, and in a way it was good that they should be. Any other girl, she had no doubt, would if only for the sake of her own dignity have given Terence up as a bad job long ago. But the prospect of life without him was so depressing to Myra that even now she wasn't quite able to face up to it. There had been no break, no scene. Perhaps there wouldn't be any, unless she made one. Perhaps Terence considered that everything had ended already, just quietly. It was sad—sad that Terence should be as he was. She was ashamed of him for being so: what was the matter with him? Why wasn't he a man? Myra was ashamed of herself a little, too. For she knew she was going to put her pride in her pocket once more and call Terence again. Just once again. Then . . .

CHAPTER SEVEN

Back with Cynthia from a pleasant round of night-spots in the company of the di Cesares, Zug began his usual lamp-extinguishing progress around the living room. "What's this?" he suddenly demanded. " '*Minor Transmigrations of the Latin tongue, with particular reference to some recent translations of the Aeneid into Sardinian, Romansch, and Provençal. . . .*' Good God, Poopsie—what is it?"

Cynthia trailed over and took a look as Zug leafed through the manuscript in wonderment. "Oh, did Terence forget it? He was taking it to be bound, or something. This gives me a chance to look at it." Cynthia laughed. "I'll read little bits before our next Latin lesson."

Zug chuckled with her. "That will give him a shock. Unless he knows about you. Does he? Does he know you've got a mind like a camera?"

"I don't think so. The subject's never come up, so far as I know." Cynthia glanced through the thesis. "I'll just read the first few pages, and then some scattered bits here and there. Footnotes too, I think. It'll be a kind of cute surprise."

"Hope I'll be there for the performance," said Zug. "No kidding—are we really going to have him around much? An absent-minded professor?"

Cynthia took his arm as they moved toward the bedroom. "Now, Zugie. Don't talk to him if he makes you nervous. Nobody expects you to talk to him. Just be nice to him, will you, please? It's for Iris, remember. We hope it won't take long. . . ."

Cynthia and Liz had indicated to Terence that Iris was naive and ingenuous. But was she? Was she *still*? She had been once—no question about that. For one thing—ludicrous thought!—Iris had been sure that all her dreams were coming true when she'd married Zug, a number of years before.

All her classic, chinchilla-trimmed dreams that she'd never thought of trying to conceal from anybody— dreams that she'd revealed in her every motion, in her very appearance, as frankly and fully as she'd revealed other aspects of herself in those shows she appeared in. Those little shows below Fourteenth Street that the police kept closing and to which men like Zug kept coming back as soon as they opened again, as they always did open again.

Zug gave up Liz for her. Not that he'd have let anybody say a word against Liz, one of the finest and most gorgeous women God had ever made: a few years before she had been as fresh and dewy as Iris, performing on the same stage that Iris was performing on now. It was just those few years that made the difference: there was beginning to be a hint of the stately about Liz's looks, and Zug wasn't quite ready for that yet. He was as generous as Liz was obliging. During and after the proceedings he floated her in all the West Seventies style he'd accustomed her to, gave her all the time she needed, and before too long the Conte di Cesare turned up, eager to add her to his collection of beautiful things.

The di Cesares moved across the park, and the Zugs did the same, and over beside the East River the whole tone of things quickly changed. With Liz taking on quite a patina as a Contessa, and with society people and high-class Italian-Americans mingling at Cesi's parties (Cesi was pronounced "Chazy," of course), amid the metal and glass furniture, it didn't take Iris long to catch on. To get rid of the dubious, cochineal-colored "Bokharas," for example, and the golden oak china closets and curio cabinets that had come across the park. Quite soon the Zug apartment, which had previously been somewhat haphazard in its contents, somewhat *criard*, emerged from the decorator's hands a refined Georgian. So very refined that young Penn-Gillis, having asked Iris at Cesi's one night if he might come to "tea," was somewhat to his surprise literally served just that the next afternoon, from a silver service.

Zug came in toward the end of the afternoon and he too, with only a few involuntary grimaces, drank tea. That would have been unthinkable a year or so before.

But by now Zug had an office in the Street, and since he was making even more money than he'd made in the days when he did his business in Times Square cigar stores and hotel lobbies, he was inclined to greet every change that came along, even the most unlikely, as an improvement. It was that attitude on his part that made it easy for Iris to tell him, a month or so after the tea party, how she felt about Penn and how Penn felt about her. Zug offered them a big wedding in the apartment, but Penn wouldn't let Iris accept; he was too impatient, he told her, to wait until she could fly back from Reno—he wanted to be out there with her and marry her as soon as the ink dried.

Penn was a sweet-looking fellow. About nineteen, anyone would think, with his yellow curls and blue eyes; Iris wished she could have seen him in his sailor suit during the war. It was obvious that he'd never look much older than nineteen, either—he was about ten years older right now. The minute she'd first caught sight of him, with his beautiful manners, Iris had known how naive she'd been to think that a man like Zug could ever be the realization of her dreams.

As a husband Penn was darling, too. Particularly after he fell off his horse during a polo match in Aiken.

They'd flown straight to Aiken from Reno, and Iris met all the Penn-Gillises. During the next few weeks Penn wasn't as aware as she could have wished him to be of the atmosphere in the big Penn-Gillis house with the stables and the camellia gardens. "They're just getting used to you, sweetheart," he said, soothingly. "Give them a little time—they're not used to anybody as beautiful as you." It was certainly true that weather-beaten old Mrs. Penn-Gillis and Penn's hard-riding sisters and cousins weren't beautiful. And they didn't try to make up for it by being agreeable, either. They didn't exactly bend over backwards to help Iris fit in. Not that they could have done much: she hated riding, and in Aiken what else is there to do? She was pretty desperate. Then one morning they carried Penn into the house on a shutter.

When the doctor told him he'd twisted his back and would never ride again Iris burst into tears—not of sorrow. The next day they flew north together with a nurse and a doctor. It was sweet and cosy living without the family in the big house on Fifth Avenue, even if the housekeeper was grumpy about having her winter rest interrupted. They gave a few parties in Penn's bedroom —the biggest was their Social Register party, given to celebrate the Register's decision to include Iris rather than drop Penn, which was what it had looked as though it was going to do before Zug, out of the kindness of his heart, got a public-relations man—that was what he called himself, anyway—busy on the people who made the Register's decisions. Iris went out dancing with friends every now and then, since Penn was strapped to a board. She had Penn's permission, naturally. Her mistake lay in presuming on that permission—stretching it to cover other things that poor Penn couldn't do, at the moment. How she cried and apologized when she found out that Penn knew! But alas—his heart had been hardened against her: for by this time the family had come north and was in the house too, and it was they who had set the operative on her trail and showed Penn his report. Yes, she had made a bad mistake, and Penn, still strapped to his board, flew to Reno, this time without her.

And now, a new winter beginning, he was back with the family in Aiken, a bachelor again, unstrapped, sitting in the sun getting strong.

The Penn-Gillises naturally thought they'd won.

They'd have been very surprised if anyone had told them that Iris didn't agree. Such was the case, however: Iris had been bitterly self-reproachful, but not for an instant had she considered herself permanently Penn-less. Beginning the very day that Penn told her his mind was made up about the divorce, she'd started having long talks on strategy with Liz. And especially with Cynthia.

For by now Cynthia had entered the scene and taken Iris's place in the big Georgian apartment, and The Three existed: a tight, harmonious little club. Cynthia was different from Iris and Liz. Zug, with his changing tastes, hadn't found her in the same little "theatre" where he'd found the others. No—Cynthia was a real actress, a real musical-comedy person, accustomed to playing roles and having conversations with other people on the stage, instead of just making a few remarks to the audience out of the corner of her mouth between taps, bumps, grinds and other movements. The others marveled at how clever she was, especially at expressing herself. She had a slight tendency to be bossy, but she was smart enough to realize that both Liz and Iris had come a long way on their own: with one of them a Contessa and the other in the Register, she knew better than to try to put on airs. They made a resourceful trio.

CHAPTER EIGHT

When he arrived at his office the morning after his birthday monologue at Ramsay's, Terence found waiting, pacing up and down in the hall, a pre-engineering student named Sanmartin, a dark, good-looking young fellow whom he knew as something of an enthusiast. Although a senior in the college, with a full schedule of courses to follow for graduation, Sanmartin had at the beginning of the term asked permission to sit in on Terence's graduate Vergil seminar. He had, he said, partly in courses and partly on his own, read every known line written by Vergil; in the army he had always carried a copy of Vergil with him; and this year, his last before entering the School of Mines, he longed to read all of Vergil once more with a guide, or at least, since he had no time for preparation, visit a course where all the poems were discussed. Terence was himself too great a lover of Vergil to refuse, and unlike most sitters-in Sanmartin had displayed a great regularity in attendance, not once absenting himself. This morning it was clear that he had something on his mind.

"I know I've paid no registration fee for your seminar, Professor Kelly," he began, almost before Terence had had time to take off his coat. "I just sit there free as your guest. So I suppose I have no right to take up your time like this by talking about it. But I couldn't resist coming to tell you how impressed I was by what you said yesterday."

Terence smiled a little deprecatingly. His seminar the previous day had followed immediately after the departmental meeting in which he'd been told of the acceptance of his thesis; and in an excess of satisfaction with his choice of profession he had found himself launched, quite without intention, upon a blowing eulogy of the Latin language, Latin literature, and Vergil in particular. Considerably to his own surprise he had heard himself telling the class how fortunate he felt himself in being able to spend his time with them in their delightful occupation of reading Vergil. Capacity for enthusiasm was one of Terence's assets as a teacher, but this time he had caught expressions of mild astonishment on a few faces in the classroom, felt he had gone a bit far, and smilingly apologized for his outburst. Now he did so again.

"Good heavens, sir, please don't apologize," Sanmartin said. "It was one of the most inspiring things I ever heard in my life. I haven't been able to think of anything else since. I scarcely slept all night, and came here first thing today to talk to you about it. You see, it's just about made me decide not to go to the School of Mines after all. I think it's given me the courage to chuck the whole thing and go in for a career like yours."

Terence looked grave. "A serious matter," he said. "Be sure you're right before going ahead."

"Oh, I'm quite sure I'm right, sir. I have no doubts whatever. I've been wanting to chuck the mines for a long time, and your remarks finally clinched it. Only . . ."

"Yes?"

". . . my father will be awfully interested in this, sir."

"Interested? I think you once told me your father's an engineer, didn't you? I imagine you'll find him a good deal more than just interested. You haven't talked with him about it yet?"

The boy shook his head. "That's one of the reasons I'm here, sir. I wonder if you'd do us the honor of having dinner with us some night. If Father could become acquainted with you I'm sure he'd take a more favorable view of my plan than he would otherwise. Maybe this Saturday? Would you by any chance be free then?"

Only the ringing of the telephone prevented Terence from instantly declining. No dinner at the Sanmartins, naturally: surely the boy would understand a professor's unwillingness to allow himself to be used in an affair of this kind.

"You've probably got someone there," said Myra's voice, "so I'll make it short. Shall we have dinner Saturday?"

Terence had thought himself well prepared to meet efficiently whatever move if any Myra might make, and had rehearsed various answers again and again for use in such a contingency, but now as he heard the pleasant voice and pictured Myra sitting in her room at her telephone, confusion set in. "I'm sorry, but I've just made another Saturday arrangement," he blundered.

"Something's come up I'd love to ask you about," said Myra.

Terence said nothing—forced himself to be silent much longer than was comfortable.

"Terence?"

"Yes?"

"You did hear me, didn't you?"

"Yes."

"I see. Well—good-bye, then, Terence."

"Good-bye."

Myra hung up first—gently. Then Terence did the same.

That was all there was to it.

"I'm awfully glad you can come, sir," Sanmartin said, quickly. "It will make a big difference, I'm sure."

There was no way out now. Terence took what precautions he could. "You mustn't give your father the impression that I'm advising or even encouraging you in your change of plan," he said. "You'll make that clear to him, I hope?"

"Oh yes, sir. All I want him to do is to meet you. I know he'll admire you tremendously."

Place and hour were agreed upon, and Sanmartin left.

So the end of Myra had come! Come by telephone! It was too soon, Terence supposed, sitting rather glumly at his desk, to feel anything but uncomfortable about it. . . .

CHAPTER NINE

Miss Quinn was sadly aware that things weren't right between her two favorite young people. On his return from overseas, Terence had taken a room in her house, and a little later Myra came too, and installed herself in what had been the front parlor, where there was plenty of room for her piano and her harpsichord. Miss Quinn spent much time there at Myra's invitation, telling her what Terence had been like as a boy. Miss Quinn had quickly come to love Myra. She thought of her as a niece, even though nothing definite was ever said about Myra-Terence arrangements.

And then Terence had moved away, into a room in one of the university dormitories. A dormitory, when he could live in the same house—the same room, practically —as his girl! That move had caused Miss Quinn's opinion of Terence to drop considerably—so much so that she was more grieved than surprised by his birthday behavior. Almost anything unfavorable, she felt, might be expected of a man who deliberately moved to a dormitory: she couldn't imagine Gus doing it under any circumstances.

She and Myra had come to avoid the subject of Terence. But the morning following his birthday, she heard the girl sobbing in her room, and after hesitating a moment she knocked. Myra let her in and they fell into each other's arms and cried. "I know I ought to stop loving him," Myra sobbed, "but I don't seem to be able to. There doesn't seem to be anything I can do about it."

Miss Quinn thought of plenty of things that she might say to Myra: "I'm sorry for you, my dear, being fond of a man who moves to bachelor quarters and won't spend even part of his birthday with his old aunt. I'm afraid I can't believe there's much happiness in store for you with a boy like that. Even if he is my nephew, I think you'd do well to forget him, if you can." But she said none of those things, and just patted the girl and soothed her.

"If you'd only known how sweet he was in Paris, Aunt Kitty. Buying me thoughtful little things all the time even when there was almost nothing in the stores, and telling me everything that was on his mind and letting me tell him what was on mine. . . ."

Miss Quinn felt a jealous twinge at that: with her Terence had always until recently been sweet, but always reserved.

"Over there we seemed to have everything in common, Aunt Kitty. But over here . . . I can't understand what's happened."

Miss Quinn could only say that she didn't either. After a while she showed Myra the draft of her letter to Mount St. Margaret's and they wept some more. Everything seemed to be breaking up for the two of them.

CHAPTER TEN

Helene-Chapeaux's telephone was of the coin, pay-as-you-go variety. She'd had the other kind at various times in her business career, but service had been discontinued so often—so regularly, almost—for non-payment of bills, that the telephone company had finally made the change. So that when she regained consciousness around dawn, that Thursday morning, she was unable to telephone to a doctor because she was in no condition to look for a nickel. All she could do was to drag herself along the floor, open the street door with a tremendous effort, call out weakly, and collapse.

A startled milkman, after glancing around the deserted street for assistance and finding none, lifted her, battered and bloody, into his truck and drove to a hospital. "Boy, was this one ever beat up good!" the orderly exclaimed admiringly, as the burden was borne in and laid before him; and indeed the patient was found to have a skull fracture and a concussion, in addition to heavy bruises without number. By the time the milkman, having given the little information he could, had resumed his deliveries, a doctor and nurses were at work; and shortly thereafter the police were in the millinery shop. They admired the shambles of the living quarters behind it almost as much as the orderly had admired the shambles of Helene herself, and after making notes they closed the place behind them, leaving it as found.

During the afternoon the patient regained consciousness, and was greatly excited by the arrival of policemen at her bedside. When one of them asked for the name of her assailant she shook her head violently—just the thing she shouldn't have done, considering its condition. From time to time she mumbled a few words, most of them incomprehensible, but a keen-eared nurse, who caught one phrase which was repeated several times, had the wit to jot it down. About dusk the police came in hopefully again, but the patient had just died, and all the nurse could give them was a slip of paper bearing the words "just a dirty lying jerk with a thesis."

They stared at it, and one of them asked the nurse what she supposed it meant.

"The way she said it," the nurse replied, "it sounded like 'Justa doidy lyin' joik widda teesis,' but I happen to know this is the way you write it."

"You mean you're from Brooklyn too, but you're educated?" the more alert of the officers asked.

The nurse nodded, giving the intelligent young man a glance of esteem. Then attendants arrived to move the body to the morgue.

Shortly after sunset a powerfully built but disintegrated-looking individual with red hair made his way out of one of the gateways of Central Park along Fifth Avenue in the lower Sixties. Carrying a gay, bouncing cluster of balloons attached to a cord, he crossed the avenue and walked steadily east. On Second Avenue he turned south for a block or two, and his steps slowed as he passed the entrance of the Hibernia Bar and Grille, but then they quickened and took him as far as Fifty-Seventh Street and then east again. As he approached a millinery shop, his steps slowed once more. But again they quickened: for he saw that the shade in the door of the shop was drawn, and that directly outside stood a policeman. After only a hasty glance, the balloon vendor turned his eyes straight ahead in the direction in which he was going, and kept them there. At the corner of First Avenue he bought a newspaper, and then made his way to the small square at the very end of the street, overhanging the river. By now darkness had fallen, and the place was empty of children and nurses who might have bought balloons, but he stood there a while, looking for something in his newspaper by the light of one of the lamps. Then, when he'd found it, he threw the newspaper down and moved thoughtfully over to the iron railing, with the space and lights of the river beyond and the rumble of the traffic on the great bridge overhead to the left. After a few minutes, still bearing his balloons, he walked up York Avenue and turned off into one of the Seventies. His steps slowed as he neared the middle of the block, and finally he stopped still, looking across the street. Boys were playing foot-ball. "Anybody been looking for me, Slats?" he called to one of them. There was inquiry among the ballplayers, and when Slats answered "Nope—nobody been around here, Red," he crossed the street and disappeared, balloons and all, into the grimy entrance of a tenement.

CHAPTER ELEVEN

For the second morning in succession a lady's voice greeted Terence when he answered his office telephone. "Professor Kelly? Terence? You're so *mean!* Do you always make your girls run after you?"

Iris! He would have called her later in the day, and he

told her so. He didn't say that he'd wanted to call her the day before, but had thought it more decent to wait twenty-four hours after ending with Myra.

"I meant what I said about making a habit of me," Iris said. "And I loathe delay. Couldn't you begin now, perhaps? I'm feeling awfully lonesome at the thought of lunch."

Terence groaned at his luck. Lunch! With a class ending at ten minutes of one and a seminar beginning at ten after two. . . . And one couldn't quite feel justified in cutting a class merely to lunch downtown, even with someone as beautiful as Iris. "If you'd take a taxi up here we could have a bite at the Faculty Club," he said, hesitantly. "Of course it's not very good or exciting, but . . ."

"I'd adore it, Terence. I'd be fascinated to see where you work and live. . . ."

He taught his twelve-o'clock class of undergraduates much less patiently than usual.

At the club, Iris was only a few minutes late. She arrived on foot, panting and contrite. "I'm so sorry, darling. I took the subway—I've really got to be careful about taxis just now, and I didn't know it was going to be so far from the station. Do forgive me, will you?"

Terence was touched. The subway was no place for Iris. Poor glamor-girl! Not the kind of person one liked to think of as being short of cash. The Faculty Club was scarcely the most suitable setting for her either, it soon became apparent. Lady instructors and professors dress better, on the whole, than they used to, but they still look different from people like Iris. They did considerable staring at her, at her little sable cape, at the bunch of paradise feathers or whatever they were that shot right up out of her yellow hair without seeming to be attached to any hat. Terence's male colleagues stared

too, but it wasn't the furs or the feathers that they
drifted over to be presented to.

Professor Hall, chairman of Terence's department,
permitting himself a kind of *droit de seigneur*, was the
first to ask whether he might draw up a chair. "A professor?" cried Iris, in tones of disbelief. "*You?* A *teacher?*
I should have said a banker, an executive of some kind.
You look so . . . so unmusty!"

"A teacher nevertheless, dear lady. A teacher for forty
years, grown old in the service of . . ."

"*Old!*"

Quite a few professors came to the table. Several drew
up chairs. After being presented to Iris they couldn't all
talk with her at once; and Terence chatted with his colleagues more than with his guest. Throughout it all, Professor Hall remained in his position of vantage, and
Terence overheard snatches of Hall stories that classes
had been hearing for forty years. "You have no idea of
the vast number of bits of all kinds of ancient marble
that one used to be able to pick up in the Roman
Forum, Mrs. Penn-Gillis. Why, limiting ourselves to one
morning's search Mrs. Hall and I on one occasion collected enough to be made into a kind of multicolored
mosaic top for a coffee table. I used to bring it to class
as a demonstration. But—and this is the point of my
tale—it's become a good deal too heavy of recent years
for my feeble . . ."

"*Feeble!*"

"You know it seldom snows in Rome. On one occasion Mrs. Hall and I were enjoying the rare experience
of walking through a snowfall in the Eternal City when
we suddenly came upon the famous figure of Marcus
Aurelius, with his golden hair all whitened. Our sentiments on that occasion were reproduced rather flatter-
ingly and neatly by Mrs. Hall in an epigram which she

composed on a later occasion, when she noticed that the poll of someone well known to her for years—ahem!—had, in its turn, become rather heavily thatched with white. 'Romana nives embellit . . .' Or, if you will permit me to translate . . ."

"How *sweet!*"

Ramsay came into view, and Terence called him over and presented him. Iris gave him her dazzling smile, but he looked away, shy and preoccupied. "Apropos of what we were talking of the night before last, I've been reading the Church Fathers," he murmured to Terence, a look of frustration on his face. "Absolutely nothing about mousetraps in any of them, so far. . . ."

He and others drifted away. It was time to leave. "I was just going to suggest to Mrs. Penn-Gillis that if she wished to have an intimate view of university life, and if she cared to do such a thing as visit a Seneca seminar . . ."

"That's awfully good of you, Professor Hall. But it does so happen that her whole reason for coming uptown was to sit in, for some reason best known to herself, in my Vergil seminar. . . ."

Professor Hall bowed. "*Senectus juventu inclinat. . . .*"

Terence found his seminar even more interminable than his earlier class, for before it was half over Iris began to stifle yawns. Two o'clock was a yawny hour for a seminar or for anything else. Terence's pupils often yawned. Sometimes he yawned himself. Nobody was bothered by it. But to make Iris yawn! Terence was in torment. Several times he considered early dismissal, pleading an appointment, indisposition. But he lacked the courage. There would be too much surprise. Somebody would notice or suspect something. Already at least one person in the room was paying Iris a good deal of attention. Young Sanmartin, the other visitor, sitting near her in the back of the room, was casting her a series of appreciative glances. No, better not let the period be marked by anything unusual. Sweat it out, as the saying went. One after the other, Iris daintily screened a series of yawns that were like a series of reproaches.

When the bell finally rang, Sanmartin stopped at the desk. "It's all set for tomorrow night, sir," he said. "Father looks forward to meeting you." Terence didn't know whether he imagined it or not, but a new kind of respect seemed to be visible in Sanmartin's glance.

Iris said the class had been lovely but that now she'd like a cup of coffee. In the drugstore she smiled happily. "You have some awfully attractive-looking students."

Terence was surprised to hear it. He'd always thought graduate Latin students about the tackiest of all. "Really? I'd have said that young Sanmartin sitting next to you was the only decent-looking one of the lot."

They strolled across the campus to Kingsley Hall. "I'm sorry, but I can't show you my room," he said, as they sat smoking on one of the leather sofas in the lounge. He hesitated a moment, then recited to her the order that had been posted and flouted in the lobbies of Army hotels in Paris: "Members of the armed forces and attached civilians are forbidden to accompany members of the opposite sex above the ground floor of this hotel." For a moment the words evoked Madeleine so vividly that he almost felt her beside him. Iris squeezed his hand. "I live in a nasty difficult kind of place too," she murmured, almost inaudibly. "So what are we going to do?"

Terence felt breathless. "I'll try to work something out. . . ."

They sat there for a while, saying little, just looking at each other. "How divine your eyes are," said Iris. "So

blue and . . . and sweet. . . ." Terence said something
—he scarcely knew what—about *her* eyes. Then he
walked with her to the subway. She wouldn't accept
taxi-fare. "You're darling," she said. "But the subway's
not bad. Really not. The worst thing about it is the way
it reminds a girl of the old days. Someday I'll be up to
taxis again. Don't worry about me. Please." She blew
him a kiss as she disappeared.

Back in his office, alone, Terence set to work correct-
ing papers, but soon found he wasn't accomplishing
much, and took up the telephone and asked for a number. "Aunt Kitty? How are you?"

"I'm all right."

"I've got something to ask you."

"Have you?"

He bristled: offended possessiveness had no place in
the new program, and his aunt would soon have to realize it. But he persisted politely.

"I find I don't like the dormitory after all, Aunt Kitty.
I want to move. Any idea as to where I might move to?"

"You can have Myra's room after Monday. For a
while, that is."

"Myra's room? Where's she going, on tour?"

"Don't pretend you care, Terence. I don't like pre-
tense."

"Now Aunty, please. . . ."

Silence.

"No other suggestions, Aunty?"

"Not a one."

"Well, thanks anyway. See you soon."

There was a break in the voice at the other end of the
wire. "Terence—don't hang up. What's the matter, dear?
Is there something wrong? Aren't you really ever coming to see me again?"

"Of course I am, Aunty. I've been busy, and . . ."

"You'd better come soon, then. I'm telling you, if you're going to see me here you'd better come soon."

"Why, Aunty? What do you mean?"

"Come soon, that's all. Better come soon. . . ."

There was a sob, and the receiver clicked.

Terence shook his head. What was she talking about? He'd visit her after Monday, when Myra had left, and see. So it was a tour that Myra had wanted to ask his advice about? He wished her luck—the best of luck. But her room . . . No, Myra's room was one he didn't want.

It almost looked as though Miss Quinn had been right in what she'd thought of saying, but hadn't said, to Myra the morning after Terence's birthday—that she would be better off without him. For the next morning Max had called Myra and redeemed himself handsomely. "Would you consider playing at the Park-Yorkshire, Myra?" he asked, chuckling. "A three-months' contract? Two hundred a week? A little music in the dining-room at dinner time, and a little more in the bar after theatre? Part classical, part blues? Would you consider that, Myra? I imagine Lily White might consider it if you're not interested, so think it over, will you?"

Max was certainly a changed man this morning. On top of the world. Spirits sky-high. "I took it right out from under the nozzle of Lily's agent," he said, delightedly. "I got wind of it and rushed to the Park-Yorkshire people. When I got there they were actually talking to Lily's agent on the phone. I waved your picture and your notices under their nozzles, and—hell's balls! How about it, Myra?"

How about it, indeed? There wasn't much that needed thinking over. The Park-Yorkshire people "wanted to let the place accumulate a kind of tradition,"

Max said they had told him. They were "tired of having a constantly changing lot of entertainers come and go." The Park-Yorkshire was a high-class hotel if there ever was one. Nothing rowdy or cheap about it. Just the sort of place Myra would enjoy playing in. She was to begin on Monday. Quite a few dinners were being given before the opening of the Opera, it seemed, and the Park-Yorkshire expected a lot of people in the Grizzly Bar, as they called it, after the performance.

Myra had only one suggestion to make. Sometimes, she knew, a hotel was willing to pay part of an entertainer's salary in room-rent. That is, hotels *had* been willing to. Now, with the room situation what it was, she didn't know. But would Max ask, please? She'd be glad to move into the Park-Yorkshire right away if the matter could be arranged.

Max called back to say that he'd arranged it. The Park-Yorkshire would be glad to have Miss Drysdale as what they called a "prestige guest." Even with Myra's prestige their rate wasn't low—"Landlords are sitting on their high hats these days," Max reminded her—but Myra could pay it and have quite a little salary left besides. So that was that. The contract was all ready. Myra had better stop in Max's office after lunch and sign it.

She invited Miss Quinn out to lunch, ordered cocktails for them both, and told her the news. There were congratulations, and a few more tears. . . .

CHAPTER TWELVE

Red hadn't been very good even when he was little. He'd always had an antipathy for telling the truth, and that had kept getting him into trouble. His mother beat him most of the time, and the rest of the time she boasted to the neighbors about his vivid imagination. Now she lived in the Incurables' Home on Tenth Avenue, if you could call it living, and prayed for Red night and day. Not that she'd seen or heard of him in years. She didn't know whether she was praying for a living son, or for the repose of a soul, but she kept on praying. There wasn't much else that she could do any more anyway. Red had grown up in the streets, chiefly, and one day he'd got himself a job of some kind and that was the last she'd heard of him. She hadn't been too sorry when he'd gone off on his own—he'd been too touchy and queer for anybody to live with. There'd never been any father—that is, even Red's mother had no idea who he was. How could she tell?

Maybe that had had something to do with Red's lying, with his touchiness, with his hitting the drink, with the fights he got into all the time. A prickly character, Red. Helene should have known that—should have known he wouldn't respond reasonably when she told him about not holding the jerk who'd come in about a binding. "Hold him, Red? How could I? How could I make him wait two three four hours? Was it my fault if he didn't come back?"

"You'd a held him if you loved me, wouldn'cha? Here, sweetheart. Take that. And that. And that."

"Red! Red! RED!"

There were only business places, deserted at night, around Helene's shop. Otherwise somebody would have heard the noise. Not only this time but previous times. But especially this time, for this time was the loudest. Red was beginning while still young to lose his strength, but as Helene knew—sometimes to her joy but more often to her sorrow—he still possessed a good deal of it. He didn't hold back this time. Yes, this time was the noisiest. And much the bloodiest.

It was the matter of blood that had worried Red after he'd seen the drawn shade and the policeman and had read in the newspaper that this time Helene hadn't been able to take it. That was why he'd stared at his house a while, and quizzed the kids, before daring to go in. He knew he'd got the blood off himself all right—but had he left any of it in his room or in the bathroom? That question had become an important one. He searched for bloodstains rather frantically when he was finally upstairs, and then calmed down when he'd made sure there weren't any. No, no traces of Helene on him or in his house.

But what traces of him were there at Helene's? That was important, too. His fingerprints were all over the place, no doubt. How would he explain them? He wouldn't deny that he'd been a frequent visitor—just that he'd been anywhere near the place that night. He'd left no other traces, he hoped. Helene had grabbed hold of him during the fight, but his clothes didn't seem to be torn, he wasn't scratched: he didn't think the police would find wool or skin or anything under Helene's fingernails. And he'd hit her chiefly with a bottle, and it hadn't broken, and he'd carried it away with him and it was safely destroyed. No: only his fingerprints in the shop were a danger. And even they were a danger only if the police had a way of learning whose they were. Had they? So far as he knew his prints weren't on file anywhere; he'd been lucky, for all his fights and sprees, in keeping away from the police. So perhaps, since the police hadn't visited him yet . . .

The thing to do was to keep from leaving fingerprints about in the future.

CHAPTER THIRTEEN

Mr. Sanmartin prided himself on knowing how to talk with men in all walks of life. He was all urbanity with his son's professor as they sat over cocktails before dinner. "Tell me about your thesis, Professor Kelly," he suggested. "What was its subject, may I ask?" Oh yes—he knew what to say to a dweller in the academic world, just as to anyone else. It was easy to learn how to ask the right questions.

And when he heard what the thesis was about he beamed. It was a subject he was far from ignorant of himself. "When I was a young fellow in Mexico, Professor Kelly—I wasn't born there, but went there quite early—I remember hearing . . ."

Jack had seldom heard his father so expansive as he was that evening. Mrs. Sanmartin joined the gentlemen for dinner, and immediately thereafter, as was her custom, disappeared as silently as she had come. Her husband talked on and on, quite fascinatingly, really, about Catalan, Albanian, and other lesser-known Latin tongues he had heard in the course of his engineering wanderings all over the world. Professor Kelly was clearly not bored at all. He even asked Mr. Sanmartin's permission to make a few notes, jot down a few expressions. "You may not know it, Mr. Sanmartin, but those Sardinian proverbs you've just given me could serve as the basis for an excellent article in the *Journal of Latin Studies*," he said. Mr. Sanmartin bowed courteously. "Please," he said, "I beg you to make whatever use you wish of these poor scraps from my memory-book. I am only a rough engineer, but I should be glad if . . ."

Yes, from the beginning it was a successful evening. During dinner Jack was tempted so often to exchange smiles of pleasure with his mother that he resolved not to look at her at all. For Mr. Sanmartin sometimes had a way of becoming sarcastic—sarcastic was a mild word to use—about "this touching mutual understanding between mother and son," as he called it. All occasion for sarcasm must be avoided this evening. The matter in hand was too important.

Terence hadn't been prepared to find the Sanmartins quite so rich: a student's invitation seldom took one to a Park Avenue apartment, especially so vast a one as this. He was indeed not bored with his evening. Of course he'd been in a good mood when he'd arrived, and that had counted for something. Who wouldn't have been in a good mood after the kind of telephone conversation he'd had that afternoon with Iris?

He'd rung her up, finally. "Hello, Iris. I'm moving tomorrow. I just wanted to give you my new address and telephone number."

"Ohhh. . . . Good. But I don't think I'll bother to write them down."

"Why not?"

"Well, after all, I'm going to be your first guest, aren't

I? And you'll probably call for me personally, won't you? So what do I need your address for?"

"But the telephone—in case something comes up. You know—about my picking you up Monday night for the Opera."

"*Monday!* Today's Saturday and you won't be seeing me till *Monday?* Just because you're moving? Are you serious? So methodical! But you're right, I suppose. Move, get settled, and then we'll . . ."

And so on. It hadn't plunged Terence into gloom, exactly. The flat he'd found to move into seemed like a good one, too. A nuclear physicist was being called out to Los Alamos for a few months, and through the university housing bureau Terence had got his walk-up.

Young Sanmartin had apparently been as good as his word, and had said nothing that could involve Terence with his father. Not once during the evening was there mention of the boy's plan to change his career. Had he told his father even of his love of Vergil, or of his visits to the seminar? There was no way of knowing. Hospitable and interesting though Mr. Sanmartin was, Terence couldn't help but feel something a little glacial about him. Something a bit cold-bloodedly self-centered, especially when he mentioned his son. He stated quite dogmatically that he considered it a father's duty to direct his son's course in life. "My son, who is following in my footsteps," he said once or twice; or, "My son, who will soon be an engineer like myself." The boy made no reply whatever to such phrases, either by word or by facial expression. Terence was glad that *he* wasn't Mr. Sanmartin's son, if there was to be a crossing of wills.

CHAPTER FOURTEEN

At the meeting in which Terence's thesis had been accepted, one of his colleagues had expressed malicious satisfaction—suitably disguised, of course, as polite regret—that his text seemed to indicate unfamiliarity with a certain rare Latin theological treatise entitled *Hieroglyphica*, the work of one Gersonius, a mediaeval Walloon. "A fascinating thing," he said, when Terence admitted ignorance. "Filled with the most striking Walloonisms, vivid examples of provincial Latin transmigration. I must confess surprise that you shouldn't be acquainted with it." He enjoyed his little triumph, and Terence humbly thanked him, being well aware of the advisability of allowing one's colleagues to score occasional innings, particularly when they're the judges of one's work.

He was aware, too, that his colleague would sooner or later expect to receive evidence that his information had been acted upon; and on Sunday, before moving his belongings by taxi from Kingsley Hall to the atomist's flat, he visited the library to read Gersonius. When he displayed his stack-permit to the attendant behind the loan-desk, he was surprised to be handed a small flashlight: the library's corps of pages, he was told, the employees who sought books in the stacks and delivered them to the loan desk, had formed themselves into a union and were on strike; and pending decision of the delicate point whether the privileged holders of stack-permits, who sought their own books, were strikebreakers, the strikers had pulled the stack light-switches and were guarding them. The stacks were in darkness, and the stack elevators were halted.

Holding his flashlight before him Terence descended on foot from level to level in the cave-like darkness. It was always quiet in the stacks, but today the stillness was profound. Here and there the faint beam of somebody's torch glowed in the pursuit of knowledge, and on the twisting stairs Terence brushed shoulders with one or two dim ascending forms whose lights were firmly directed, like his own, not on the faces of passers-by, but, for safety's sake, on the steps themselves. In the remote sections of the sub-sub-basement that housed Latin theology all was stillness and blackness, and flashing his light on the call-numbers posted on the ends of the long aisles of shelves, Terence slowly made his way toward Gersonius, *Hieroglyphica*, 774.9 Ger 95. Once in the proper aisle the beam of his light played along shelf after shelf; he bent, then crouched—Gersonius was shelved close to the floor. His light moved jerkily along: 771, 772 . . . He was almost at his goal when he heard soft footfalls, and approaching his aisle from the other end he saw another flashlight-beam.

The wielder of this beam was clearly more familiar than Terence with the stacks containing the 770's: very smartly, not hesitantly like Terence's, the light came toward the aisle, then entered it and approached him. Beginning at the top shelf it moved quickly down, and at the very moment when Terence's beam of light finally played on 774.9 Ger 95, the other beam played on it too. Like an enemy aircraft, Gersonius was caught in the crossbeam, but this time it was not the prey, but the wielder of the other light, who was the enemy. There was a sharp intake of breath, and as Terence's hand went out to the volume there was an indignant cry: "Stop! That's mine!" In his astonishment Terence glanced up, forgetting that he could not see; the lights were still directed at the book, and the figure beside him remained in darkness. During the moment it took him to remember to raise his light, the cry became a snarl of rage, and the crier dealt Terence's other hand a sharp blow, knocking the book to the floor. Then his beam revealed his assailant. "Ramsay!" he cried. "Ramsay!" And to his dismay, his host of a few evenings before, abruptly ending his horrible, animal-like snarl with a kind of sob, sank into a chair that stood beside the research table at the end of the aisle and buried his head in his arms.

Appalled, Terence could think of little to say or do. He made a pool of light by standing the two flashlights upright on the table, and he pulled a chair up to Ramsay's and spoke as soothingly as he could. "Shall I get you some water, Ramsay? Rest here a bit. Then come and lie down in my room. Take it easy. Take your time. Just be quiet. . . ." Ramsay made no reply. He lay sprawled over the table, breathing convulsively at first, then more normally. After what seemed to Terence an eternity he slowly lifted his head and raised himself so that he sat slumped in his chair. "Terence," he said finally, in a voice that was his own but tired, "can you manage to forgive me?"

"Forgive you for being ill? I'm worried about you, Ramsay. Do you think you could come with me now, and lie down someplace?"

"I'll be all right," said Ramsay. "Quite all right again, I think. Thank you, Terence."

And after another moment of sitting quietly he took out of one of his pockets a crumpled slip of paper bearing a number. "Page reference," he said. "Would you open?"

Terence retrieved the fallen volume from the floor and

opened to the proper page. He found at once, by the light of the flashlights, what Ramsay had been seeking. From the middle of the page the words seemed to stand out—a quotation, the text said, from Saint Augustine: "*Muscipula diaboli, crux domini*. The cross of our Lord was the devil's mousetrap," he read aloud. "Is it the solution of your mystery, Ramsay? A kind of parable? Does it mean that St. Joseph made possible, even in his passive way, Christ's birth, which of course had to precede His death on the cross? In other words that St. Joseph, the carpenter, constructed the mousetrap that caught the devil? Is that it?"

"That's it, of course," said Ramsay, his eyes beginning to brighten a little. "That explains the *presence* of the mousetrap, at least. But it doesn't explain its absence from the fourth panel. Why in the world, I wonder . . ." He sat there, pondering the mystery. Already, it was clear, the recent unpleasant scene was receding, for him, into the distance.

But when he tried to copy the quotation his hand trembled, and Terence did it for him and put the book back on the shelf. Then together, Terence carrying the two flashlights, they climbed out of the stacks and left the library.

Ramsay refused a taxi, and refused to go to a drugstore or to Terence's room. "I'm quite all right again," he said, snappishly. "Quite all right, I assure you." Terence referred no more to the episode, but walked him to his door.

"Why do *you* think the mousetrap disappears, Terence?" Ramsay asked, as they parted. "What ideas have you about it?"

But Terence had no ideas about mousetraps.

Back at Kingsley Hall he lost no time telephoning the office of the university physician, and the nurse on Sunday duty gave him the doctor's home number. The university physician might never have heard of Ramsay, of course: many campus people went to doctors of their own. But there was a chance. Terence telephoned and asked permission to call, and arrived at the nearby apartment house in five minutes.

Yes, the doctor did know Mr. Ramsay. He shook his head at Terence's story. And Terence's heart sank, for the doctor said he was not surprised. He was surprised only that Terence himself should have been so surprised: evidently he hadn't been seeing much of Mr. Ramsay lately. Ever since the beginning of the term grotesque behavior on Mr. Ramsay's part had been all too frequent. Sudden laughing fits in class, loud monologues in public halls, fits of abstraction during which he was oblivious of his company. . . . The university was concerned, deeply concerned. It was the university authorities who had referred Mr. Ramsay to the doctor. He had seen him several times. This was the first instance of behavior that could be called violent. The doctor thanked Terence. Something, he feared, would have to be done quite soon. . . .

CHAPTER FIFTEEN

But even thoughts of Ramsay's Sunday behavior faded on Monday night, at the Opera House.

Terence's only regret, as he sat in his chair in the back of Cynthia's box, was that he didn't have a *front* view of The Three as they sat there on display: people in the other boxes seemed to be enjoying the triple half-length no end. Cynthia wore a mass of diamonds just under where her Adam's-apple would have been had she had one. Not a diamond necklace, exactly—there weren't any diamonds wasted on the *back* of her neck; just a big lump of them in front, like a marvelously glittering goiter, held in place by a platinum string. How they blazed, off and on, in the dimness of the Opera House, catching fire from the gleam of lights in the boxes! Quite a few people kept watching for Cynthia's diamonds to catch fire, instead of watching *Rigoletto*. During the entr'acts, they watched Liz's emeralds. In the bar, as newspaper photographers flashed their bulbs, people came close, stared at the incredible stones as they lay on Liz's stately chest, and went quietly away again, feeling all the better for the experience. Iris looked modest beside Cynthia and Liz. Still glamorous by Faculty Club or almost any other standards, of course, in her beauty and her sable cape and her features. But jewelless—quite jewel-less. "She gave everything back," Liz whispered to Terence. "Everything. Imagine!"

Zug sat beaming in his chair as only the sight of The Three together, particularly in the evening, could make him beam. Wall Street was full of operators with two divorces and a third wife. But Zug! (This was the way he imagined, at least, people talking about him.) That Zug! Such women! What a picker!

And then the Conte di Cesare . . . This was Terence's first meeting with the Conte. It would scarcely be exact to say that he occupied the sixth chair. It was his, but he was out of it most of the time. Mostly he sat under one of the lights in the little anteroom, cleaning his nails. He seemed extraordinarily nail-conscious. Once he caught Terence's glance and nodded to him in a friendly way, holding out all ten of his fingers like exhibits. "Wormhole dust," he called out, explanatorily.

"What can I do? Wormhole dust, day after day. . . ."
He didn't lower his voice at all, and it boomed out quite loudly. Some of the people in the neighboring boxes seemed surprised to hear the words "wormhole dust" suddenly shouted during the performance, and looked around to see where in the world they'd come from. But the Conte was invisible, hidden in his anteroom. He emerged for an occasional aria. Sometimes he even sang one. Not that he always knew the words:

> La donna è mobile,
> Ta-ra-ra boom-de-ay. . . .

The Conte had lived in America for generations, Cynthia had told Terence one day, and the quantity of antiques he'd smuggled out of Italy in his lifetime would have furnished a city of palaces. He seemed to have quite a singing voice despite his age and his long exposure to wormhole dust. A few protesting hisses came from other boxes as he sang his arias, but he paid no attention. After they were over he applauded vigorously, shouted "Bravo!" or "Brava!" as the case might be, then retired to his nail-cleaning.

Liz kept uttering cries of appreciation. "Ah, Carusissimo! Ah, che sopra-Tetrazzinismo! Ah . . . !" She was hissed, too. "Aren't hissers the futilest things?" she demanded aloud, of no one in particular. "Don't you pity them?"

In the bar, during the entr'acts, Zug treated to champagne. He didn't treat only his box-guests. Anyone who came up to greet any one of The Three, or Zug, or the Conte, was handed a glass of champagne by Zug's waiter just as though it were a party in the Zug home. And indeed, especially during the second entr'act, that was what it came to resemble: Zug was host to a goodly assemblage by the time the warning bell rang. Some of the Conte's friends were picturesque: veteran Italian-American opera-goers in antique coiffures and musty evening gowns, looking as though they had stepped out of the chorus of *La Traviata*. There was much hand-kissing, much exclamation of "*Gia!*", much flitting of fans. "*Fans!*" Iris whispered to Terence, her feathers quivering with her laughter. "*Fans!*"

There was even somebody at Zug's champagne party who had come up to greet Terence: young Sanmartin, looking darker and more distinguished than ever in his white tie and tails. He called Terence's attention to his father, standing some distance away, and the men exchanged bows. Terence introduced the young man to Iris, and the three of them stood chatting, sipping their champagne. Then Terence excused himself briefly, and went over to utter a few words of thanks to Mr. Sanmartin for their interesting evening the previous Saturday. "You do have such nice-looking students," said Iris, as they moved back to the box after the warning bell.

The last scene of the opera delighted Zug. At the tragic climax he slapped Cynthia on the back, making her diamonds blaze out more brightly than ever. "It's in the bag!" he chuckled. "In the bag!" What with his exclamations, and the Conte's intoning the last fatal chords with the orchestra, and Liz's murmurs of "*La maledizione!*", the indignant protests from adjoining boxes were pretty well drowned out.

Out in the street Zug told everyone to get into his car. "Send your man away, Cesi," he ordered. "My man will take us where we're going. We'll all stay together a little while longer. Can't break up the party as early as this."

They all piled in, and when the car drew up under a canopy they all piled out again, and went inside. Zug led them to a bar where somebody was playing a piano.

"Now," he said. "Nightcaps for everybody." And when nightcaps appeared he ordered "Bottoms up!" And then, almost immediately, "More nightcaps!"

The words "Bottoms up!" and "More nightcaps!" seemed to be Zug's formula for the evening: he uttered them commandingly and unceasingly, and everyone obeyed. And then he said, "Scrambled eggs—how about it? Scrambled eggs, folks? How about you, Professor—scrambled eggs?"

It was just after he'd said yes, he would have some scrambled eggs, that Terence became aware that the unusual-sounding piano being played at the other end of the room wasn't a piano at all, but a harpsichord, and that Myra was playing it. And before he'd had time to do more than vaguely register the fact, something else was beginning to happen. Something fantastic. Cynthia was reciting his thesis. Reciting it!

"Listen to this, everybody," she said, holding up her hand. And when they were all listening she began: " 'The recent almost simultaneous appearance—somewhat unexpected, it must be admitted, considering the temper of the world about us, and all the more gratifying for that—of new translations of the *Aeneid* into Sardinian, Romansch and Provençal, gives an unlooked-for sense of timeliness to any attempt that may be made to re-examine the structure, and the present-day employment, of these minor but always interesting offshoots, or rather descendants, of our great Roman mother-tongue. Such an attempt, in the opinion of the present writer, may not improperly be called overdue; for not since the pioneering works of . . .' " Cynthia quoted the first two paragraphs of the thesis exactly, in a very solemn voice, and then she recited the footnotes to each paragraph in proper order and without a single mistake.

"What in the world . . . ?" said Liz, forgetting her

Italian for the moment. And Iris said, "Cynthia darling, are you sure everything's quite all right?" Zug was grinning, and the Conte's monocle was gleaming in wonderment.

Cynthia pointed to Terence. "Isn't he sweet?" she said. "See him blush—as though it weren't his due that somebody pay him a little tribute, after all that hard work. We didn't have nearly enough of a party at my house the other afternoon for you, Terence—not nearly enough of one, considering it was both birthday and thesis day. Consider this your thesis party, Terence darling. Here goes, everybody: pay attention to Chapter Five!" And then she recited a passage which was indeed from Chapter Five, all about the eccentricities of modern Albanian, with the same perfection of performance. The only difference was that her voice was a little shriller now.

Terence was blushing indeed, as everybody congratulated him. All raised their nightcaps: "To Terence's thesis!" Zug not only drank, but informed Terence emphatically that he should feel honored, *honored*. "I do," Terence assured him, his head spinning. "Indeed I do. Thank you all, very much."

"You should," said Zug, thickly. "It's the most unique tribute *you'll* ever receive, Professor. I hope you realize that."

"*Molto delicato*," confirmed Liz. "*Delicatissimo*."

And all during Cynthia's recitations and during the congratulations and the toasts Terence heard the harpsichord tinkling away at the other end of the room. Through the buzz of voices came bursts of applause whenever Myra finished a piece, especially one of her blues pieces, which sounded particularly wistful on the ancient instrument. Myra was too far away to be able to see him, but even so Terence would have preferred to be elsewhere. "Don't you want to go?" he murmured to Iris. "Aren't you tired?"

But just then Myra played a fanfare on the harpsichord, and the maître d'hôtel or manager or master of ceremonies or whoever he was stood up and said there would be a little dancing—an innovation in the Grizzly Bar. Just a few minutes of it, he said, as a very special exception "to honor the first night of Miss Drysdale's engagement." A little floorspace was being cleared, and anybody who wanted the unique experience of dancing to a minuet played in swing time on the harpsichord . . . There was a burst of applause, and Iris said, "Oh, Terence darling, wouldn't that be fun?"

But Terence shook his head in a kind of panic. He was no dancer, and besides—dancing with Iris, up there under Myra's eye and to Myra's music . . . And he had scarcely shaken his head, and said "Oh no, I don't think so," when out from what was now, after all the nightcaps, quite a haze, loomed somebody who was certainly young Sanmartin, and who bowed to him politely, and bowed to Iris, and said "If you're not dancing, sir, perhaps Mrs. Penn-Gillis would dance with me?" And Iris said, "Oh, how nice! Just a minute or two, Terence dear, and then you and I'll be off," and she and young Sanmartin were on their way to the dancefloor, and Myra began a Mozart minuet, swinging it ever so slightly, and there was more applause, and laughter and cries of pleasure from the direction of the music.

Young Sanmartin! Why in the world should *he* turn up again? And then as Terence stared out across the room to watch Iris dance a minuet with him, if he could watch anything with his head spinning as it was and everything running together so, he caught sight of somebody else: *old* Sanmartin, again! Standing there in the entrance of the room looking the place over as though he owned it! The Sanmartins! Why in the world should they be in the Grizzly Bar? But Mr. Sanmartin was there only briefly. He disappeared even while Terence stared. And after a while the minuet ended and the dancers came back. "Thank you very much, sir," young Sanmartin said, and Iris asked the boy to forgive them for not asking him to sit down, but they were just going. He bowed politely, thanked them both again, and disappeared.

Despite the protests of the others, Terence and Iris said good-night. "I don't want you ever to forget that compliment, Professor," said Zug, and as a kind of farewell Cynthia chanted: " 'Chapter Nine. Modern Galician. The northwest corner of Spain is, one may say with no fear of contradiction, an anomaly of anomalies in modern civilization. Here, living much as their forefathers lived ten, if not twelve or even fifteen centuries ago . . .' " And as they moved away she called out, across other tables of nightcappers, "See you at the Latin lesson!" The other nightcappers in the Grizzly Bar seemed almost as surprised at that as the people in the opera boxes had been at hearing "Worm-hole dust!" shouted from nowhere during *Rigoletto*.

"All those nightcaps!" said Terence in the taxi. "I'm sorry if I seem a trifle dazed."

Iris said she didn't mind.

"I'll be better shortly. You're coming with me to see the flat, aren't you?"

But Iris admitted that the nightcaps had been a touch too much for her, too, and said she thought she wouldn't come up this time, though she "had planned to."

Terence urged her a little, but she shook her head.

"Be sweet, Terence. You *are* sweet. And your students do dance divinely."

They said good-night at Iris's door.

Far too many nightcaps undoubtedly, but the evening had been worth it, hadn't it? So amusing, except for Myra's presence in the Grizzly Bar. Terence lay back in the taxi with all the windows open, letting the cold air revive him on the way uptown. More than ever the new program seemed the thing. Once again, rather groggily, he went over his inauguration of it on his birthday: classes in the morning, The Three in the afternoon, Ramsay at night. So safe! Avoidance of his aunt's reproaches, the final decision about Myra. . . . And already, if only it hadn't been for the purely extraneous factor of night-caps, Iris would be coming home with him. Iris, the evening in and out of Cynthia's box—those were but indications of the sort of delightful, non-involving activities the program was going to make possible. . . .

The maître d'hôtel in the Grizzly Bar was beginning to be uneasy. One of the tables was getting a good deal noisier than he liked. He didn't want to do anything to offend Mr. Zug—Mr. Zug came in often, and brought people and spent money—but tonight Mrs. Zug was so shrill. What nonsense she was talking! Shouting, rather. Almost screaming. "Listen to this, everybody! Listen carefully! 'That fascinating offshoot Catalan, too, is deserving of our attention. For more, perhaps, than any of its brother and sister tongues which we have been considering, it preserves . . .' Out of a thesis, folks! Straight out of a thesis by my friend the Professor. He left it at my house on the way from the binder's, and little did he think when he did so, my friends . . ."

Somebody was approaching the Zug table now. Somebody who had been standing at the bar. A guest of the house. Every so often one had guests of that kind, looking things over, or just dropping in to enjoy themselves.

They weren't particularly welcome, and they came less often to the Grizzly Bar than to many another establishment. There was no reason for them to come at all: the Grizzly Bar was quietly elegant and respectable, except for an occasionally jarring note like Mrs. Zug. The maître d'hôtel walked quickly over to see what the guest of the house was up to.

"What were you saying, madam? About a thesis? And a binder?"

Mr. Zug had jumped to his feet. He'd been running up too much of a bar bill, apparently, to notice the quick flash of the badge. "What's it to you?" he demanded. "My wife's got a mind like a camera, but what's it to you? Who are you, anyway, butting in like this? You're acting like a flat-foot."

The badge flashed again. "That's what you might call me, mister. And if you wouldn't mind telling me what you were saying just now, madam, about a thesis and a binder, it would save a lot of embarrassment and trouble all around."

The maître d'hôtel came up quietly. "Won't you all come into my office? We'll have some drinks there, and everything will be much more private. I'm sure Mrs. Zug said nothing that she won't gladly explain."

The maître d'hôtel glanced gratefully at Miss Drysdale as he escorted the Zug party and the guest of the house out of the Grizzly Bar. Her harpsichord was rippling and roaring, entrancing everyone. Neither she nor anybody else, except those directly concerned, seemed to have seen or heard anything amiss.

PART TWO

CHAPTER ONE

The Giulianos lived on Spring Street. Not because it was near Mulberry and the rest of that Italian neighborhood—indeed that was in their eyes one of the disadvantages of Spring, for they lived very much to themselves and despite their upbringing they in no way considered themselves Italian or as belonging to any Italian colony. No, they lived on Spring Street rather for two other reasons: because they had found a cheap little flat there and because it was in a very different part of town from the orphan asylum. Joe and Sadie had both been raised in the big Italian orphanage up near the Stadium; they had both gone to Public School right in the orphanage building, and lived in the building while going out to High School. Joe even lived there while going to craft school, though Sadie was gone by that time, living in the Nurses' Home. They had spent enough time in, or even near, the orphanage, they both felt. When they married they didn't care to live where they would be apt to even see it. So they looked for a flat downtown and found the one on Spring Street, and into it they gradually put books, gramophone records (almost ostentatiously not restricted to Italian music), and other possessions. It was a cosy little place, and they were happy there for several years.

There was a dispensary up the block, and the day his

summons for induction came Joe stopped in without saying anything to Sadie and had himself measured in his socks. During the weeks the induction card had been expected, Sadie had measured him several times herself, standing him up against the bedroom wall, and every time she did it she felt cheerful: for the lowest result she could obtain was six feet six and three-quarters, and twice it came out six feet seven. Since the army's topmost limit was six feet six she was considerably reassured. "How can they take you?" she kept saying. "They'd have to make you special shoes, special clothes, special beds. . . ." Joe was inclined to agree with her, even after the visit to the dispensary. "Six feet six-and-a-half, mister," the orderly said. "How's the air up there?"

In his earlier years Joe hadn't been easy on wits who asked him how the air was up there. He'd snapped at them, like a dog at flies. "Fine! How is it down around your ———?" was one of the milder retorts he'd been in the habit of making, and more than one skirmish had resulted. Joe had usually won: he'd been one of the orphanage boxers and knew how to make use of his long reach. "Wanta come up and find out, shrimp?" was one of his variations, accompanied by a lifting gesture toward the scruff of the questioner's neck. But he seldom said anything like that any more. Joe had mellowed. At thirty he regarded people who asked him how the air was up there as a species of distasteful insect fulfilling their natural function. It was Sadie who had worked the change: she'd hated the scenes that sometimes resulted from Joe's retorts. "Look at those Golden Glows," she said during their honeymoon, after a scene in a restaurant that had embarrassed her horribly. "See how they're pestered with red bugs? You really can't blame the bugs, you know. Think of yourself as a Golden Glow, just for my sake. Be as nice about the bugs as you can."

"I'm a Golden Glow," Joe had retorted the next time somebody asked him the question in Sadie's presence. "Just a god-damned Golden Glow. Golden Glows don't bite, and that's the only reason I don't bite *you*—see?"

Sadie started packing a bag as soon as they got home that night, and said she wasn't going to live with anybody like that any longer. "How old are you?" she asked him. "Five? Ten?"

Joe sometimes complained that she'd broken his spirit, but he had to admit that he was all the happier for not letting pests get under his skin. He had a few other rough spots, too, that Sadie smoothed down, and their life together was better all the time. That was why Sadie kept measuring him: she never pretended to be unselfish about the draft.

The six feet six-and-a-half in the dispensary was a quarter of an inch less than Sadie's lowest result at home, but Joe had confidence in his remaining extra half-inch when he went to the Grand Central Palace induction center. Sadie was on night duty at the time, and came home just as he was leaving. "I'm not sure I'll do much sleeping this morning," she said. "Come back and take me out for lunch, will you please?"

It all happened fast at the Palace. "Hundred ninety-five pounds," the medic called when Joe stepped on the scales. And then: "Six feet five-and-a-half. How's the air up there?"

Even if he hadn't given up making retorts Joe wouldn't have been able to think of one just then. "You mean *six*-and-a-half, don't you?" he gasped. "That's what I was yesterday."

The medic looked sympathetic. "Diddums shrink a whole inch over night, just because oo was scared of nasty Selective Service?" he inquired. "You're still too tall for the Navy, bud, but I think I can assure you the Army will be charmed to welcome you."

For a second Joe glared and tensed his long arms. Then he shrugged. "You people must need men pretty bad to cheat a fellow out of a lousy inch," he said. "So I'll take pity on you. What the hell. . . ."

The medic winked, and said "Next!" and that was all there was to it.

Joe never confessed to Sadie how easily he'd surrendered. Their lunch that day wasn't a cheerful one, and the next two weeks weren't cheerful either. Mr. Crane, the head of the binding department at Boswell's Bookstore, shook Joe's hand when he left and told him that naturally he'd have his job back when he returned—"if there's still a binding department at Boswell's, and you know there has been for a century,"—and before long Joe was writing Sadie that army clothes seemed to fit him quite well except at the wrists, that army shoes, far from pinching him, were more comfortable than any he'd ever worn before, and that the only thing he had to complain of was the length of army cots—apart, of course, from the separation from her.

It turned out to be quite a separation: three years, during which they didn't see each other a single time. Sadie lived alone in the flat and went out on her cases just as before. Then Joe came back from various Pacific places, thinner, and with some of his old rough spots back and a number of new ones. Sadie had to re-do some of her work on him. But she didn't mind that: now they could both begin to live again.

Living again presented certain difficulties, because of what Mr. Crane had to tell Joe. He was sorry about the change that had taken place at Boswell's. The century-old binding department had been given up, temporarily at least. Leather was scarce, the vogue for fine bindings seemed to have declined. He himself was being kept on only because of his long connection with the firm, and only until he could find another position. "I haven't found one yet," he said, "and I've been looking for quite a while. Good luck, Joe—I'm afraid you'll need it."

Mr. Crane was right about that. There didn't seem to be a binding job in New York. After a depressing month or two of hunting, Joe began taking samples of his work to small stores in well-to-do neighborhoods and offering the storekeepers commissions on any work they could get him: he had his own press and tools at home, and could work there. Nothing came of it: not a single order from the little bookshop off Park Avenue, from the stationery store opposite Carl Schurz Park, or from the millinery shop near Sutton Place. Joe was like an actor in not wanting to take a job outside his line, but he had to eventually. He was no scholar—he didn't know very much about the inside of books; and he wasn't much of an artist—he wasn't one to originate designs. What he could do was a good clean job of binding, copying any style or motif that he was shown. He liked the feel of leather. The army had been rather puzzled as to what to do with him, and had finally put him to work servicing trucks. Now he took a job in a taxi terminal, servicing cabs. He'd have been bitterer than he was, if Sadie hadn't been so clever about flattering him and if they hadn't been so happy to be together again.

And then things got better. Mr. Crane was by now teaching binding at a settlement house, and when enrollment grew heavy he got Joe to help him, teaching a few classes a week. And about the same time there was a telephone call from the bookshop saying that a gentleman wanted to talk about having a set of magazines bound. It turned out to be not one set but several, and it led to other jobs for the gentleman and his friends, and once again Joe was earning his living as he wanted to. He and Sadie started a baby—a bit imprudently, perhaps, with everything costing so much—and Sadie stopped working. "I hope people start leaving us alone now," Joe said, shortly before the baby was due. "After those three years, and after that taxi garage, I hope people will start leaving us alone. . . ."

Neither of the Giuliano's happened to read the little item in the paper telling of the death of the proprietress of the millinery shop near Sutton Place.

CHAPTER TWO

Under ordinary circumstances nothing would have pleased Myra more than what she read about herself in the night-club column of the *Times* on Tuesday morning. The paragraph was entitled "Where Did You Get That Harpsichord, Lily White?" The *Times* night-club reporter must have done some quick checking with somebody from the record company: he'd scarcely have risked the libel action that Lily would certainly have brought had his facts been wrong:

"We had a drink in the Grizzly Bar of the Park-Yorkshire last night, and listened to Myra Drysdale begin her engagement there. Such playing! It's a precious experience to be sent by a harpsichord, and only Miss Drysdale has ever given it to us. She's done it before, and last night she did it again, looking her pleasant self as usual. Lily White *almost* did it, in one or two of her new records, which we recently heard, but only almost. And by the way, if you want to do a little detective work, listen to one of the White records just before or after hearing Miss Drysdale: not only to hear two contrasting ways of playing, but—unless we're wrong, and we bet we're not—to hear two contrasting ways of playing *on the same harpsichord*. Next time Miss White records, we suggest she use her own instrument: feeling at home with it might make just the important difference. Meanwhile we emphatically recommend Miss Drysdale, who can be heard nightly for some time to come, we're glad to say, in both classics and blues. And how about an album of records by *her*, record company gentlemans?"

"How you feeling this morning, Myra?" Max demanded joyfully over the telephone. "Any complainings?"

"None at all," said Myra. "How about you, Max? How do you feel?"

"Fine, fine—fine like a fiddle. . . ."

The Park-Yorkshire people were pleased, too, and sent up more flowers to Myra's room—as though they hadn't piled enough of them on the platform the night before; and a number of friends telephoned congratulations, among them Miss Quinn. After lunch Myra went into the Grizzly Bar, a closed and dreary room at that hour, and practised. She cried a little in the deserted place. If only Terence were around, to make the success of her opening a pleasure, instead of just a new job that was beginning well!

After practising a while she went to the news-stand and bought the afternoon papers, to see what they might have to say about her.

CHAPTER THREE

Terence wasn't enjoying himself either. Neither a hangover nor an arrest is pleasant, and they're especially unpleasant when they happen together.

"Howja expect to get away with it, Bud?" his cellmate kept asking him. "A teesis! You sure signed your own det' warrant, usin' a woid like dat when you was goin' around moiderin' dames. . . ."

And from across the corridor someone kept groaning "Oi, oi, oi, oi . . ." until Terence thought he'd go crazy. Every once in a while, indeed, he wondered whether he *was* crazy, whether he was really spending this Tuesday morning in a detention cell instead of in his office and his classrooms. A detention cell! "We'll do everything possible—if anything *is* possible—about bail and so forth later in the day," the Inspector told him. "Meanwhile of course you're perfectly free to consult an attorney, but I consider it my duty to warn you that everything will be much simpler if you don't."

Around noon, when Terence was beginning to pull himself together sufficiently to suspect that despite the Inspector's words it would perhaps make things considerably simpler, for him at least, if he *did* consult an attorney, he was taken out to see a visitor—a gentleman with a brief-case who introduced himself as Mr. Harwood, the Public Relations Officer of the university. "This is a horrible thing, Professor Kelly," he said, in an aggrieved tone. "A horrible, horrible thing."

Terence agreed that it was.

"If only they hadn't come for you to Kingsley Hall!"

Mr. Harwood lamented. "If only they'd gone straight to your apartment! That would have been so very preferable, from the university's point of view!"

"I suppose it would," Terence replied, his frayed temper betraying itself in a certain vocal edginess. "Are you reproaching me for not having *expected* to be arrested— for not having furnished the police with my new address in advance, out of consideration for the university?"

"Well," said Mr. Harwood, "some of the headlines wouldn't be *quite* what they are, probably, if you had." And he mutely held out for Terence's inspection the front pages of various afternoon papers. Terence found it impossible to suppress a groan when he read: "Latin Prof held in Modiste Murder," and "Thirty-year Dorm Record Spoiled, Mourns Murder Suspect's House-Mother."

"Of course it's typical journalistic inaccuracy to call Mrs. Peebles a house-mother," Mr. Harwood said scornfully. "You know Mrs. Peebles—that fine elderly lady in the Kingsley Hall office, in charge of the mail and so on. Her real title's Office-Manager. The reporter obviously either didn't go to college, or else attended some provincial institution where for all I know men's dormitories may actually be equipped with house-mothers. Mrs. Peebles is due to retire next year, and she's naturally upset about the police coming in. It makes her feel she's ending her career under a cloud. Well, you see what you've done to the university's good name, Professor Kelly. Tell me: do you intend to resign? That's always the cleanest way. A statement in the newspapers saying merely: 'University authorities announced today that Professor Kelly, murder suspect, is not a member of the teaching staff,' would close the affair immediately as far as the university is concerned. If you've decided to resign you might as well tell me now and I won't come here troubling you any further."

"Did Professor Hall ask you to come here and say that to me?" Terence demanded.

But Mr. Harwood seemed unable to place Professor Hall, and when Terence explained his identity he was clearly astonished. "The chairman of your department? Heavens—so far as I know, *he* plays no role whatever. An upper-level matter like this isn't handled by professors. It automatically becomes the concern of the university's highest administrative echelons. I should have thought my presence here would have told you that," he said, looking offended. And when Terence told him that he had no intention of resigning, that the whole thing was a ludicrous error which could be cleared up very easily, Mr. Harwood sighed. "So it's that kind of a situation, is it?" he said, wearily. "I was afraid it might be. You plan to go on and on, getting yourself exonerated and dragging the university's name through the mud?"

It was at that point that another visitor was announced: Miss Quinn. Her eyes were red, but she wore a defiant air. "How can they hold you on this ridiculous charge, Terence?" she demanded, in a voice so loud that all of headquarters could hear. "Haven't you told them that you spent the entire evening and night of the murder with me? Where would you be likely to spend the night of your birthday, except with your old aunt, the only bit of family you've got in the city?"

Terence smiled, and introduced Mr. Harwood, and told her not to worry and not to pretend. "The night man at Kingsley Hall saw me when I came in around midnight," he said. "The police say the poor woman got her beating considerably before that, and I've got good proof of where I was."

Mr. Harwood rose. "Well, since you're not resigning the only thing for me to do is to phone an attorney and have him drop in here to see you," he said. "Have you an attorney of your own?" Terence shook his head, and Mr. Harwood said he was glad of it. "We prefer cases like this to be handled by people we know, people whose first concern is the university's interest," he said. "I imagine Slade and Slade, the university's attorneys, will consider it to the university's advantage to get you out of here as rapidly as possible, though of course I can't swear to it. When they come and see you, you might make a suggestion to them along those general lines, and see if they agree."

Terence assured Mr. Harwood that he would, and the Public Relations Officer took his leave, the lack of consideration shown the university by its employees clearly oppressing his spirit. And then Miss Quinn did some more worrying, and a little sobbing, before the policeman on duty told her that her visiting time was up and she'd have to go.

Back in his cell, with "Oi, oi, oi, oi," coming from across the corridor at monotonously spaced intervals, and with his cell-mate asking him whether the date for his trial had as yet been set, Terence composed himself as best he could to wait for the visit of Slade and Slade. In the newspapers left by Mr. Harwood he saw that apart from his admission that he had visited the millinery shop, no details of the information that he had provided during his questioning had been released by the police. There were merely photographs taken after his arrest, and "human interest" stories, more or less facetious according to the newspaper in which they appeared, about the spectacle of a professor of Latin in the toils of the law. Terence was grateful that from journalists and police alike he had been able to conceal the extreme heaviness of the hangover he had been suffering at the time of his arrest.

A third visitor was shortly announced: a young man who presented a card bearing the name of a law office that was not Slade and Slade. He had once handled a legal matter for Miss Drysdale, he said. As soon as Miss Drysdale had read the afternoon papers she had called him up and asked him to put himself at Professor Kelly's disposal. So here he was. What could he do? Terence thanked him, but sent him away.

And very soon thereafter the Inspector who had been in charge of his questioning came to his cell, had a policeman unlock it, and told him he was free to go. "Slade and Slade gave me a ring," he said, obviously impressed. "They don't usually bother with cases of this kind, so I'm giving you the benefit of the doubt, even if the milliner did mention you practically in her dying breath. I can't say you've been very helpful to us."

Terence thanked him and stepped into the corridor. "Would you mind telling me," he asked, "whether anybody else has been arrested in this case?"

"What do you want to know for?" said the Inspector. "What makes you think anybody but you might be arrested?"

As sometimes happens, it was only after asking his question that Terence fully realized why he had done so. "I was just wondering," he said, "whether you'd happened to pick up that binder. She told me she expected a visit from him that very night, you know. I did mention that to you this morning, didn't I?"

The purplish color that the Inspector's face suddenly turned, and the rather frightening heaviness of his breathing, told Terence that in the hungover condition in which he had undergone his questioning he must, incredible though it seemed, have omitted the detail.

"If that attorney's call had been from anybody except Slade and Slade I'd push you back in that cell with my own hands this minute," the Inspector said hoarsely, when he could talk again. "She definitely told you she expected a visit from the binder that night?"

Terence nodded apologetically.

The Inspector stared at him as he had never been stared at before. "Well?" he roared, after a moment. "*Come on.* I'm waiting. Come on with the rest of your delayed recollections."

But try as he might, Terence could add no more, and, finally, feeling the Inspector's stare boring into his back, and wafted along by a steady breeze of outraged reflections and epithets, of which "——— ———— ————————" was by far the most printable, he walked out of headquarters.

CHAPTER FOUR

Liz, whose apartment was to have been school the next day, telephoned the others as soon as the evening papers were out. "That skunk!" she said. "There won't be any more lessons, needless to say, so why wait till tomorrow to get together? Come over here this afternoon for a drink, why don't you?"

As early that morning as they'd dared telephone her, Cynthia and Liz had told Iris about what had gone on in the Grizzly Bar after she and Terence had left; and now in the afternoon at Liz's they all went over everything again, each reading aloud bits which she thought one or both of the others might have missed.

"Professor Kelly was arrested as he was leaving his apartment house on his way to class. . . ."

"Too bad we weren't all there to see the expression on his face when the cops grabbed him, the louse."

"He had been living at this address less than forty-eight hours. . . ."

"Why did Terence move? Do you know, Cynthia?"

"No idea."

"Do you, Iris?"

"Well. . . ."

The others gasped. "Heavens! *Really?* Had you . . . ?"

Iris shook her head. "I swear. Just not. *Just.* Cross my heart. Narrow escape, though: almost went there last night."

They scolded her seriously. "Crazy! Reckless! The whole idea was for you to keep your skirts clean. Otherwise . . ."

"I know," said Iris penitently, "but we expected *so* much from him I thought he'd do the job better if I made him happy. . . ."

They shook their heads. Poor Iris! Always generous —always wanting to give something to somebody. Always wanting to make somebody happy—usually the person she was nearest to.

"So now, with all our plans upset," said Liz, "what do we do?"

But they got off onto a discussion of the crime.

"We know he's a rat," said Cynthia. "He's let us all down. But what do you think? Is he guilty?"

"I don't *think* he's guilty," said Iris. "I *know*."

"Angel! You do? How?"

"He has a killer's eyes."

"*Dio mio!* So he did it last Wednesday," Liz went on, musingly. "The night of his birthday. After we'd dropped you and Zug off that night, Cynthia darling,

Cesi and I drove right past that hat shop, you know. How I'd have shuddered if I'd known what was inside! The street was absolutely empty, I remember, except for somebody who must have been leaving a party or something, walking along at that hour carrying balloons and something that looked like a bottle. . . ."

The telephone rang just then, and to the astonishment of the others Liz waved at them and announced "Terence!" in lip-language.

Yes, it was Terence, calling to tell Liz that he hoped nothing they'd read in the papers had made The Three change their plans about the next day's Latin lesson.

"Are you out, *caro Terenzio?*" Liz asked, grimacing wildly at the others. "Out on bail, or something?"

Terence said rather stiffly that bail hadn't been required.

"I'm so glad, Terenzino. But about tomorrow I don't quite know yet. Something's come up. Call me just before class time, will you? Then we'll see."

Terence said he would, and Liz said affectionately "We're dying to lay eyes on you, darling. When *is* your trial?"

She reported with satisfaction to the others that Terence had been quite sharp in his answer to that. "There's not going to be any," he'd snapped rudely. "What makes you think there should be?" Liz made some indulgent reply, as one would to an irritable child, and said good-bye. "I'm afraid being in jail makes Terry feel he's no longer bound by the rules of common courtesy," she told them, smiling.

"Sounds to me as though he's beginning to crack," said Iris. "He'd better find a little more self-control someplace if he doesn't want to give himself away completely."

"Anyway," Liz said, "I don't think he'll like it tomorrow when none of us answer our phone and don't even leave a message for him. That's the way to treat him, I think—torture him—considering what he's done to us, especially to Iris."

Terence had no idea of what he'd done to them all. Not the slightest idea. They discussed the situation, and possible next steps, as the twilight deepened in Liz's living room and shadows fell on its furniture of metal and glass, Cesi's late-in-life revenge against wormhole-dust. . . .

CHAPTER FIVE

Miss Quinn flung her arms around Terence's neck when he appeared at her door that evening, as though he were returning from the dead or at least from a death cell. He was all the more annoyed by her emotion because Myra was there, just leaving after paying what had clearly been a consolation call. "Good evening, Myra," he said, straightening his tie. "Thanks a lot for sending down your lawyer."

Myra said that he was very welcome and that she was glad he'd got out so quickly. "Yes," he said, "it's all over, thank goodness."

Then Myra rather abruptly left for her job.

"Oh, Terence," said his aunt, when the door closed. "Myra's so sweet. If only . . ."

But Terence requested her not to say "If only," and requested her furthermore as a favor to him not to be emotional if she could help it, because he'd had a hard day, and not to question him about the day's events, because he preferred to forget them. "I'll just tell you," he said, "that the whole thing was a mistake, and that the university lawyers have such prestige that they got me out by telephone. So there's nothing to worry about. Now then—what did you mean the other day when you told me I'd better come soon if I expected to find you here? Are you going away someplace?"

"I am."

As unemotionally as she could Miss Quinn told him about Mount St. Margaret's, and as she did so she saw that he looked unhappy. "For heaven's sake why, Aunt Kitty?" he demanded. "Why in the world do you want to go into an old ladies' home? What's the matter with staying right here?"

She was afraid that her eyes might be shining, but she made a great effort not to betray in any other way her pleasure that he should care about what she did with herself. "Oh, it was different when your mother was alive and we had each other to visit," she said. "You know after you went overseas and she was lonesome she grew a little friendlier with me again. Of course she never forgave me for . . . Well, I mean she was perfectly pleasant with me as long as she had her own way about everything we did together. But then that was her way of being pleasant with everybody. You know what I mean."

Terence admitted that his mother had had a way of insisting on her own conditions.

"And then I stayed on till you came home because you wrote me you counted on living here, and it was nice having you. But with you uptown where you are, and too busy to drop in very often . . . Besides, I'm getting old, and a place like this with servants what they are today . . ."

Terence was more upset than he could have imagined

at the thought of his Aunt Kitty disappearing through the doorway of an old ladies' home, and he was on the point of saying something silly and sentimental. Then he remembered his new program—just in time. "Well, I suppose it's up to you," he forced himself to say evenly. "You must do whatever you really want to."

Miss Quinn nodded, not trusting herself to speak.

"I don't know anything about old ladies' homes," Terence said, seeking refuge in something more general, "except that I do remember Mamma talking about a case Father once had involving one. Apparently they all used to be deathly afraid of being sued by inmates' relatives. People entering homes used to turn over their money to the institution in return for being taken care of, didn't they? Or promise to bequeath to the institution whatever was left of their capital when they died? Well, sometimes relatives used to be annoyed that *they* hadn't got the money, so they sued the institution, claiming either that the person concerned had been of unsound mind when he signed the agreement, or that the institution had forced him to sign. That's why it's become a custom for old peoples' homes to ask an applicant to include the names of any close living relatives in the application for admission. Whatever the financial arrangement may be, they write the relatives, telling them of the applicant's intention. It's just a formality nowadays, coming down from the earlier situation. The whole point of the case Father had, as I remember Mamma telling it, was that the applicant who was his client . . ."

But Terence never finished his reminiscence, for he saw that heavy tears were rolling down his aunt's cheeks. "Oh Terence," she cried, "if only . . ."

"Now Auntie—I asked you not to say 'If only. . . .'"

"I *will* say it. Oh, Terence, if only you'd been here

the night of your birthday when I filled out the blank. Of *course* they asked for the names of my brothers and sisters. And of *course* I gave them. I had no idea they'd *write* to them. Oh, Terence—I'd never have applied if you'd been there to tell me they'd do that. Think what Ed and Monica-Grace will write Mount St. Margaret's about me! And May . . . !"

"Now Auntie. . . ."

But Miss Quinn burst into sobs, and Terence well understood that she should do so. There were no uncles or aunts on his father's side, but on his mother's, in addition to Kitty, were the three whom Kitty had just mentioned, all of them in a factory town near Boston where Terence had never been. As young women Terence's mother and Kitty had left to work in New York, and family ties had quickly slackened. Kitty's life with Gus, which had loosened even the ties between the two sisters in New York, had almost entirely ended relations with Massachusetts. After the death of Mrs. Kelly, Kitty had visited the others briefly, taking a few mementos with her, but the visit had not been a pleasure.

"Ed and Monica-Grace!" Miss Quinn sobbed, passionately. "Imagine what *they'll* write to Mount St. Margaret's about me and Gus. . . ."

Terence could imagine. A stained glass window in his parish church in memory of his deceased wife, a framed papal blessing in his parlor, the non-existence in his home of any plumbing except a kitchen sink even though he was a plumber himself—those, Terence knew from his aunt, were the outstanding attributes of his uncle Ed Quinn. One didn't look for much more from him. And as for church-mousy Monica-Grace, who wasn't a nun only because her widower brother needed a housekeeper . . .

"What about Aunt May?" Terence asked. "She's the

most liberal, isn't she? The most literate, too. If the others do send a letter about you they'll probably get her to write it. Couldn't you appeal to her? Isn't she more broadminded than the others?"

Miss Quinn's tears gave way to scorn. "Appeal to her indeed! May *broad*minded? Where did you get that idea? Your mother and I did use to think there was hope for May when she was teaching school—you probably remember hearing us talk about her when you were a child. But after she married that undertaker Mahony . . . Oh, by the way," she interpolated, "did I remember to tell you that May's boy, your cousin Vinny Mahony, was ordained last month? She mailed me an engraved announcement. I sent him a small gift, but I don't suppose I'll hear anything. I'd love to see him in his vestments." And then the thought of the probable letter that would be sent to Mount St. Margaret's broke through again, and tears reappeared.

There was nothing more that Terence could think of to say. Indeed, his aunt's tears, brought on by his attempt to help matters by putting the subject of old ladies' homes on a painless and impersonal basis, were but another reminder of his inability to do anything except harm by interfering. He patted her hand, and for the rest of the evening they talked of other things.

CHAPTER SIX

Red was no book-binder, of course. How could he be? The binding craft is exacting and complicated. A bum can't learn it. Not while he's a bum, at least, and

Red had been one ever since reaching the so-called age of reason. And although a bum can be regenerated and become almost anything, nothing of that sort had happened to Red.

No—stevedoring had been Red's first work after he'd left his mother and gone off on his own. But his habits hadn't been regular enough for stevedoring. The effects of his nights before became too serious. Other stevedores were injured because Red had the shakes and couldn't carry his part of the load. He became unwelcome on the piers. So he took to hanging around the warehouses on West Street, picking up cartons and boxes that the warehouse people threw out and selling them for what he could get. There were fights over the cartons: quite a few characters like Red were generally hanging around to grab them. Red could fight, all right. He usually got the cartons he wanted. And then he somehow drifted into balloon-selling—lighter, more agreeable work. Stevedoring, carton-scavenging, and balloon-selling: those had been Red's occupations. Those and lying. Lying had always been his steadiest work—especially with Helene.

Passing her shop one day on his way to sell balloons in the little East River park, he'd caught a glimpse of her through the glass and stopped to stare. She'd stared too, and smiled—the mistake of her life. Red saw the bindings and the sign saying that orders were taken, and he went in. "I'm a binder myself," he said. "I'm a binder when I can get the work. I can do better than any of *that* stuff."

It was an ardent hour or so, passed chiefly on the other side of the dirty portieres. From the very beginning Red refused to believe, or at least pretended to refuse to believe, that the binder's arrangement with Helene had been a purely business one—that is, purely would-be business. "I swear to Gawd," said Helene, "I swear to Gawd that man never laid hands on me."

"You expect me to believe that, honey?" said Red, showing her vividly just how incredible he found it. Red was at his sweetest that day—his sweetest and gentlest. Helene was enraptured. He said he'd bring his business cards the next morning, and some samples of his work.

He didn't, of course. He'd discovered, he said, when looking around at home, that all his best binding jobs had been sold. He had none on hand except a few that weren't up to his highest standard. He'd get some more ready as soon as he could, and bring them in. As for business cards—he was out of them, too, and it took much longer to have them printed nowadays than it used to. In the meantime, would she mind leaving her other gentleman friend's bindings in the window, just temporarily? She consented, and during the next few months Red enjoyed hearing her say, from time to time, that Giuliano had stopped in during the day to ask whether there had been any orders. "I didn't tell him that if there had been I'd have passed them right on to somebody else," Helene said merrily, and they laughed together. Red hoped that he might run into Giuliano in the shop some day: he'd get a lot of fun out of actually seeing the fellow he was tricking. But Giuliano stopped coming. Red never did see him—not while Helene was alive.

Red didn't waste any time worrying about what he'd do if an order came in and Helene passed it on to him for execution. He had a marvelous lack of ability to worry—a lack amounting practically to a gift, a gift of the sort that seems to be vouchsafed to bums as well as to saints and sages. The meals Helene cooked for him, her rapturous acceptance of the kinds of pleasure he indulged in and bestowed—these filled him with contentment, and he didn't dream of spoiling contentment by worrying. Indeed when Helene told him that someone had finally been in about a binding, and that the person had gone and not returned—even then he had no thought of having had a lucky escape from being found out. To him the situation was something else: a chance to pick a fight with Helene.

It never occured to Helene to doubt that he was the binder he said he was. Why should it? Wasn't he her dream man? Helene's dreams were rough a good deal of the time, and Red turned them into the most appropriate and satisfactory kind of reality. She believed him to the day she died. In Red's mind she died a natural death after a roughhouse that was a little rougher than usual, although he realized rather dimly that other people couldn't be expected to agree with him. Only then had he begun to worry. About blood, and then about fingerprints.

During his acquaintance with Helene he had lived a regular life, and following her death he continued to do so; but now the regular life was minus Helene, and that made a difference, considering how they had spent their time together. Balloon-selling in the park, a slick-up in the men's room at the end of the day, a stop at the Hibernia Bar and Grille—less to drink at the Hibernia these days, and a bit to eat since there wasn't a Helene any more to cook supper for him—and then home to bed. Such was Red's life these days. He thought about fingerprints a good deal. At night he dreamed of them. During the day he kept watching himself make them, and he wiped them off whenever he could: he punctured more than one balloon trying to rub his fingerprints from its surface, at the Hibernia he kept surreptitiously wiping the bar and his glasses and plates and knives and forks, and at home he wiped and scrubbed incessantly. Gradually he came to wear gloves most of the time. That left him unoccupied. He grew more and more restless and nervous. He had to *do* something. . . .

Joe Giuliano had been brought to headquarters long before Terence had ever been located. Naturally: his business cards had been found in the shop. He lost no time in making an unfavorable impression. "Somebody —probably somebody big and husky like this one—flew off the handle and beat the woman to death," the Inspector remarked to his assistants. "Maybe it *was* this one. At least, you can see how this one flies off the handle."

When the men in plain clothes had rung the doorbell of the flat in Spring Street late Thursday, the day after the murder, and told him why they'd come, Joe had been calm enough. He said that he hadn't heard of the milliner's death, and hadn't seen her for months. But when they suggested that he accompany them he got excited. "You can see my wife's condition," he said. "Have a heart and let me stay with her tonight. In the morning I'll come down and answer any questions you want to ask."

The plainclothesmen showed no signs of agreeing to that, and Sadie had to calm Joe down and tell him to go quietly. She whispered to him to keep his temper at headquarters, kissed him good-bye and told the plainclothesmen she hoped they wouldn't keep him long. "I really don't like to be alone nights at the moment," she said, and they looked uncomfortable and mumbled something.

She was alone most of the night. Joe came back exhausted and angry. "Same old question a thousand times," he said. "'What do you know about it?' What could I say? I could only tell them a thousand times I didn't know anything."

"Did you tell them politely, at least?"

"Of course I did."

"Sure?"

"At first I was plenty polite. I was polite a lot longer than they deserved."

"And then?"

"Well . . ."

When Joe confessed how exasperated he'd become and just how he'd answered a few times toward the end, Sadie wondered that there had been an end—that they'd let him come home at all.

That was Friday morning. They left Joe alone till Tuesday—until after Terence had been released. Then they came back for him. Once again he was polite at headquarters—at first. "Somebody tells us that the milliner expected you that night—the night she was killed," the Inspector said. "What do you say to that?"

"I say that somebody's not telling the truth, Inspector."

"Do you indeed? Suppose I was to tell you that the somebody in question is a most respectable gentleman —a professor, no less. Would you still suggest that we believe you rather than him?"

"Somebody's lying, Inspector. I don't know who, except that it isn't me. I was home that night. Your men can tell you I have a good reason to be home nights."

"I might as well tell you the business about your being expected isn't all we learned, Giuliano. We learned that you and the milliner weren't just business acquaintances. Our informant knows for a fact that up until a few months ago, at least, you and she were on intimate terms. . . ."

Poor Joe! He tried hard, but he didn't succeed. He

shouted rather loudly. "God damn it, Inspector, I don't believe for a minute the law says I have to stand here and listen to you give me that kind of God damn dirty . . ."

After waiting at home alone a long time, and getting more and more worried, and then telephoning headquarters, Sadie finally arrived with a lawyer from the Legal Aid Society. But by then it was too late in the day to do anything, and the Inspector was able to keep Joe overnight to teach him the "lesson in manners" he said he needed. In the morning they let him out in time to rush home before going to the settlement house, to see if Sadie was all right after her night alone.

"Just wait till I get my hands on that professor," he said, as he hurried out to work. "Just wait. . . ."

Sadie didn't scold him. People who don't know very much about their own parents, like Sadie and Joe, are sometimes more sensitive than others about the regularity of their own lives. It was bad enough for the professor to say that the milliner had expected Joe that night—that was a lie on somebody's part. But that he should "know for a fact" that Joe and the milliner were intimate. . . . That kind of a lie was something different. Sadie thought more approvingly than otherwise about Joe's idea of "getting his hands on" the professor. Indeed she found it quite easy to imagine scratching the professor's eyes out herself.

The Inspector hadn't minded at all letting the Giulianos assume that the professor, who had told him of Joe's being expected by the milliner, had also been his informant concerning the intimacy between them. The truth, the Inspector knew, would sound terribly weak: "We've received an anonymous letter. . . ."

Not that he hadn't been pleased when the anonymous

letter had arrived, that morning—the all but illegible unsigned letter with its crooked printing, telling the police of Joe's connection with Helene's shop and with Helene herself. For the arrival of the letter proved him right; and the Inspector had no more dislike of being proven right than has anybody else—a little less, if anything. "See how right I was in saying no publicity on Giuliano?" he said to his assistants. "If it had been in the papers that we'd talked to him, this person probably wouldn't have felt obliged to write us about him. Now we've got a letter to work on, at least. That's more than we had before." And he turned it over to the handwriting-analysis and fingerprint people.

The Inspector was inclined to pride himself on a flair for knowing how much publicity to give the various suspects in these minor murder cases with which the District Attorney was too busy to bother and which he let the Inspector handle himself, much to the Inspector's delight. "Now take professors," he'd said that evening, after Terence had left. "Professors are absent-minded. Everybody knows that. This one was pretty upset by those newspaper headlines, and after he'd seen them he remembered something. Get the point? He probably knows a lot more than he thinks he does. I don't question his sincerity. Just his memory. He's got to be upset some more. See what I mean?"

His assistants said they saw.

"The more trouble you can make for the professor," the Inspector summed up later, after Joe had been questioned, "the more he's likely to remember. Not only publicity. Anything you can think of. Little things. You might even check his alibi. As for Giuliano, I don't think there's anything there. What about the letter?"

The letter didn't promise to be very helpful. The handwriting-analysis people shrugged their shoulders and could say only that it had been printed in disguised hand by a man who seemed to be naturally uncouth; and the fingerprint people said that both the letter and its envelope were spotless. "For that matter," the chief fingerprint man said to the Inspector, "we might as well forget the print angle in the whole case, in my opinion. You know how it is with shops. Customers' prints all over everything. Hopeless."

CHAPTER SEVEN

At the close of the Vergil seminar on Wednesday a lady graduate student—one of those whose glasses shine so brightly as to obscure, for a teacher, everything else about her, including her name—came up to Terence's desk and began to giggle nervously. "Would you, Professor Kelly?" she asked. "Would you be so kind?" She was offering him her fountain-pen and her Vergil text, open to a blank flyleaf. "Any kind of an inscription at all, Professor. Even just your signature."

Terence frowned and hesitated for a moment, then hastily signed his name, despising himself as he did so.

"Oh, *thank* you. . . ."

As she withdrew, another suppliant loomed up on the other side of the desk. This one wriggled. "Anything you feel like writing, Professor Kelly. Just anything. . . ."

The idea caught on. Quite a few of his lady graduate students asked for his autograph before the room emptied. The men looked uncomfortable or disgusted and hurried out. Young Sanmartin was absent for the first time.

The autographing of the Vergil texts was not the first episode of the day, nor yet the last. In Terence's undergraduate class a freshman had made an unfortunate slip of the tongue while translating Tacitus aloud. He rendered *molitor* not as "miller" but as "milliner," violently embarrassing the rest of the class. And before lunch Professor Hall asked Terence to step into his office. His desk was piled with the previous evening's newspapers. "Mrs. Hall and I were wondering last night whether you would do us the honor of bringing that charming Mrs. Penn-Gillis to tea," he said. "Could you perchance come Saturday afternoon? That day is always a real Sabbatum for us, a lull after the week's turmoil. . . ." And when Terence said he would be happy to bring Iris if she was free, Professor Hall inquired, "I take it Mrs. Penn-Gillis is what might be styled 'the other woman in the case'? Or, looking at it the other way round, the milliner was 'the other woman'? The whole thing was what our French friends call *un crime passionel?*"

Those proved to be surprisingly difficult questions to answer, and Terence's explanations, which he felt the chairman of his department was entitled to, took up all the time they spent walking across the campus to the Faculty Club. By the time they reached it he thought he had made everything clear, but he was quickly disillusioned. "Kelly's just been telling me about this business we've all been reading about in the papers," Professor Hall generously undertook to say, addressing at large the other occupants of the common table at which they had seated themselves, and where an air of constraint had become noticeable at their approach. "Let me state my position clearly. The literature of the ancient world, with which I think I may claim to be reasonably familiar, abounds in examples of otherwise estimable men led to desperate deeds by an excess of one passion or another.

I hope we are all humanists here, gentlemen, in the widest sense of the word? I, at least, am not going to be the one to cast the first stone. Fate, and fate alone, is the villain of the piece."

Except in the mind of Professor Hall himself his words did little to help matters, and his cheerful farewell to Terence after lunch brought uneasy expressions to the faces of all: "Keep a stiff upper lip, Kelly. And barring change of plan my wife and I shall be delighted on Saturday to welcome you and your charming . . . er . . . accomplice. . . ."

After his seminar Terence was peremptorily summoned by telephone to Mr. Harwood's office.

"You probably wondered why Slade and Slade didn't send somebody to headquarters to talk with you, as I told you they would," the Public Relations Officer said, with practically no greeting. "You probably wondered why they just contacted the Inspector by phone, didn't you?"

Terence had not wondered, actually, but Mr. Harwood gave him no time to say so.

"I'll tell you the reason. Slade and Slade agreed with me that from the university's point of view it would be well to get you out of jail. But they were chiefly interested in their own reputation, naturally. They consented to use their prestige to call up the Inspector and persuade him to let you out, but that is absolutely all they consented to do. They declined to send anyone from their office to headquarters. They declined any further activity on your behalf. Slade and Slade are very high-class lawyers—that's why the university employs them. They dislike crime of all kinds. I don't blame them: I dislike it too. But the result is that you're without counsel, and that headquarters, because you have no counsel for them to communicate with, has taken, since just this noon, to communicating with *me*. It's most deucedly unfair. Why should they keep making threats to *me* over the telephone about indictment and all the other things they're planning to do to *you* if you don't produce a satisfactory confirmation of your alibi?"

Mr. Harwood's face was eloquent of indignation, but he was not the only indignant person in his office. "Indictment!" Terence cried. "Something's terribly wrong someplace! Without counsel! Why didn't you let me know yesterday that Slade and Slade weren't representing me? Why in God's name didn't you tell me last night . . . ?"

Mr. Harwood's voice was cold. "Kindly moderate your language, Professor Kelly: the President's office is just down the hall. And don't argue with me: it may interest you to know that I was the first man to receive a degree of Doctor of Public Relations in this country. Kindly remember that even though *you* may be interested only in *yourself* in this matter, *I* am a busy man, Professor Kelly, not always able to keep *you* informed of every last little detail concerning *you*. If you had taken my suggestion and quietly resigned. . . ."

"It's a pretty big detail to find myself without counsel in a murder case, Mr. Harwood. I've got no worries as far as my alibi is concerned, but . . ."

"Really, sir, such egocentricity I have rarely if ever . . ."

After they had both got themselves somewhat in hand, Harwood told Terence that the police were having difficulty with his alibi. They'd been ringing up whoever it was with whom he claimed to have spent the murder evening, and they couldn't get any answer, and they'd found no one at home when they'd called in person. "This," said Mr. Harwood, "seems to be making them irritable."

"Strange that there should be trouble," Terence said. "Mr. Ramsay is home so much. I gave them his home address for that reason and because that was where I spent the evening with him: I suppose it didn't occur to them that he could be reached at the university, since he doesn't have the title of professor. I know he wasn't home last night, because I called him myself to tell him I'd given the police his name, but he must be there today because I didn't see him at the club, as I'd hoped, and when he doesn't lunch at the club . . ."

An expression only to be described as one of extreme distaste had been gradually taking form on Mr. Harwood's face, as though someone had been telling an off-color story which filled him with increasing disgust, or as though he had been slowly becoming aware of a loathesome and fetid odor. "Ramsay?" he said, turning his eyes on Terence slowly and with obvious lack of pleasure. "Did you say *Ramsay?* You mean the Ramsay in the art department?"

"Yes I do," said Terence. "Why?"

"Oh, nothing," said Mr. Harwood. "Nothing at all. Except that it just happens that I had another case on my hands yesterday, in addition to yours—the case of Mr. Ramsay. So far, I've been able to keep *his* affair quiet, except from the few people who actually witnessed it, and I'd hoped I was going to be able to continue to. But I see you're out to spoil everything, Kelly. For your information, Mr. Ramsay was carted off to a booby-hatch yesterday morning. Just a booby-hatch, that's all. Just a slight case of insanity. He suddenly started talking about mousetraps or something in class, and began drawing things on the blackboard that were scarcely the kind of thing one draws in public. By the time they got him to the university doctor he didn't know where he was and began to grow violent. Your alibi's in a strait jacket someplace at the moment, Kelly. The university physician can tell you where to find him."

Liz was nettled when she telephoned the others. "Such cheek, my dear! My man says he didn't sound cool, exactly, but that he very definitely didn't express the slightest interest in us or in the class. He just said something pompous about checking an alibi. He's got a swelled head, if you ask me. All wrapped up in himself, now that he's been in the papers. He was so eager to say he couldn't come that he didn't even give my man a chance to tell him I wasn't in and wouldn't be in and that none of us would be in. *Che impudenza!* For all he knew, we were all waiting here for him to come and give us a lesson. *Che mancanza di gentilezza!*"

In Kingsley Hall, where Terence on his hasty way from Mr. Harwood to the university physician had stopped to telephone to Liz and to pick up any mail that might not have been forwarded to his flat, Mrs. Peebles broke down instantly at the sight of him. "*House-mother!*" she sobbed, uncontrollably. "*House-mother!*" Her assistant, a young woman with a set face, helped her into an inner office and came out to fetch a glass of water. "Beast!" she hissed at Terence, glaring at him on her way to the cooler. "You've ruined *every-thing* for her! Her whole *image* of herself. . . ."

CHAPTER EIGHT

"We were able to remove Mr. Ramsay's jacket last evening," the floor nurse told the university physician out in the hall. "He dictated a note that he thought he wanted sent off, and he grew quieter as soon as we pretended it had been taken down in shorthand and mailed. He slept well, and I think you'll find him in good shape." The doctor, who had accompanied Terence to the Medical Center, went briefly into Ramsay's room and then came out and told Terence he could see his friend for a few minutes.

Ramsay looked well and seemed quite happy in his little room with barred windows. His voice was normally lilting, without any of the alarming and depressing tones it had had in the library on Sunday. "How very nice of you to come so quickly, Terence," he said, cordially. "I don't see any books, though. Didn't you bring them, as I asked?"

"I couldn't today, Ramsay. Didn't have a minute. Besides, I have a confession: I lost your note."

"Don't worry. I have the titles in my head. I'll give them to you again before you go. Now let me sum up the situation. The mousetrap is identified as *Muscipula Diaboli*. We know from Gersonius—or rather from St. Augustine—why it *is* there. What we don't know is why it *isn't* there. By the way, in my note I asked you to bring the photographs. If I'm to be here for some time I want them to stare at. That's one of the best ways to get ideas about pictures, you know—just by staring. Or, as I occasionally say in class," Ramsay added with a

116

smile, "usually with astounding effect on at least one earnest youth who'd never thought of it before, the best way to learn about pictures is to look at them. That's what's known as inspiring teaching, Terence, in case you didn't know it."

Yes, Ramsay seemed quite content. It wasn't possible to know whether he realized where he was.

"Ramsay, I wanted to ask you something about last Wednesday night. A week ago today. My birthday. You remember, the night I . . ."

"Tell me, Terence," Ramsay interrupted, "how did it happen that you were looking for Gersonius, of all people, that day in the library?" Terence told him of his colleague's recommendation of Gersonius's Walloon-isms, and learned that it was the same colleague who had mentioned to Ramsay one day its mousetrap quotation from Saint Augustine. "I can't imagine why I didn't go straight to Austin myself long ago," Ramsay said. "Naturally I knew that the Church Fathers are full of all kinds of metaphors, and that religious painters made use of them in their pictures. You remember that other metaphor about the Redemption, Terence—the one that speaks of Christ's body as being bait on a sort of divine fish-hook, luring the demon to destroy himself. I'm not sure just who thought up that one: both Cyril and Gregory use it, you know." Ramsay had a way of assuming that one did know such things as that. "I mean Gregory of Nyssa, of course. Why in the world didn't I think of Augustine long ago?" he said, self-reproach-fully. "It humiliates me to have been guilty of such neg-ligence."

"Ramsay—about last Wednesday night. . . ."

" 'The devil, a Leviathan, tried to bite the precious flesh of Jesus Christ with the bite of death,' " Ramsay quoted, meditatively. " 'But the hook of divinity that was concealed within and joined to the flesh, tore open the devil's jaws and liberated the prey. . . .' Yes—that's another way the holy fathers visualized Satan's defeat. But the mousetrap image is so much richer, so much more suggestive. It puts me in mind of all kinds of little things. Scurrying little mice, little hollow places they run into . . ."

A smile that Terence didn't like the look of was playing over Ramsay's face: it made one wonder, even though one didn't want to, just what it was that he had drawn on the blackboard that day he'd lost control of himself in class.

Then the door opened and the doctor came in and told Terence his time was up and that if he'd wait for him in the hall they could go back to the university together.

"I was just reminding Mr. Ramsay that I spent last Wednesday night at his house," Terence said. "If you'd just mention to the doctor, Ramsay, the fact that I was there that night . . ."

But Ramsay assumed a sly look. "I don't understand why you keep talking about Wednesday," he said. "What are you driving at? You know quite well, since you seem determined to bring the matter up, that the day we saw each other was Sunday—Sunday afternoon in the library. And my earnest advice to you, Terence, is to say as little as possible about your behavior on *that* day. 'Unfriendly' would be a mild description of it. Snatching books . . ."

"But Ramsay—the police are interested in where I was the Wednesday before that, the night you first showed me the mousetrap pictures, and you've got to help me."

"The *police!*" said poor Ramsay, drawing himself up in bed with a fastidious air, and with even more of a lilt in his voice than usual. "I have *never* had anything to do with the *police*: why in the world should you insinuate that I might have reason to?"

The doctor was pointedly holding the door open for Terence.

"Don't forget the books," Ramsay called in farewell. "Bring me Gersonius—unless of course you still want to pre-empt it yourself—and Mone's *Lateinische Hymnen des Mittelalters,* and the volume of Bachtold-Staubli's *Handwörterbuch des deutschen Aberglaubens* that contains the article '*Maus,*' and Peter Lombard and some of the other holy fathers, and the photographs . . ."

"Mr. Ramsay's a person of real scholarly integrity, isn't he, under that unusual manner of his," the university physician remarked on the way downtown. "Whatever else you may say about him, he's not a yes-man like so many of our people on the campus. I mean—if he means Sunday he won't pretend to mean Wednesday, will he? I admire a person like that. . . ."

CHAPTER NINE

Most people found it difficult to place Mr. Sanmartin. What and who was he? Very few people knew: he didn't go in for friends or reminiscences. For years he'd been an American citizen, but he spoke English with a faint hint of an accent—an accent that seemed to come from somewhere south of the border or out in the Caribbean. He was a wealthy man—no question about that. But what business was he in? Mining, he always said;

he was a mining engineer. And that was what he did seem to have been during all the years he'd spent wandering around the world. But what was he *now*? Lately, certainly, no one had seen him near a mine. He'd long been established in his New York apartment, and his appearance was more reminiscent of Park Avenue than of a mine. He was a swarthy man, neat and well-manicured, with small hands and feet and a twirled, waxed moustache.

Jack resembled him, apart from the moustache. Some people might have said that Jack also resembled his mother: she too was dark-complected, and her features weren't markedly different from her husband's. But such a thought never occurred to Mr. Sanmartin. Mrs. Sanmartin was wife and mother. As such she had fulfilled her function and had earned the right to be supported and lodged, but she didn't count. She appeared at the dinner-table. The rest of her time she spent with women friends, shopping or otherwise inoffensively occupying herself. Mr. Sanmartin seldom thought about her, except when she and Jack seemed to have their heads together. Then he said something effective and they moved their heads apart.

Although as a small boy Jack had traveled around and around the world with his parents, he bore few marks of his foreign schoolings. There was a slight formality about him when he talked with his elders, but otherwise he had long been Americanized. That pleased his father: it was one of the many points of resemblance between them. There were so many. Even when it came to Jack's little rebellions. For years Mr. Sanmartin had been chuckling about those.

Naturally Jack was going to get a bachelor of science degree, enter the School of Mines, and after graduating from it spend a few years at some of the properties his father was still interested in—learn mining thoroughly. Not in order to spend his life in mines, of course. Just the opposite, as his father kept telling him: he was to learn mining so that for the rest of his life he could stay above ground, handle his mining interests like a gentleman, and with the income they brought branch out into any other lines he chose. That was what Mr. Sanmartin had done. Jack must do the same. He had to learn where the money came from and how it came and how to make it keep coming. Mr. Sanmartin had been able to enter innumerable amusing and profitable lines of business because he knew those things so well. The theatre business, for example; the hotel business: Mr. Sanmartin had a lot of such golden eggs. He enjoyed taking Jack to a play, and saying, "Nice theatre, don't you think? I own it, you know." Or taking him into a hotel restaurant for a meal, or a hotel bar for a drink, and telling him, as he paid the check, "Well, here I am helping pay my own operating costs—and my profits, too." Those golden eggs and a lot more like them would eventually be Jack's, once he'd familiarized himself with the goose that had laid them.

But how Jack had rebelled! More than once, and each time betraying an intensity of character that had tickled his father enormously. The first time had been during the boy's early teens, and had concerned a violin. Jack had asked for one after going to a concert with his mother, and she'd given it to him, bird-brain that she was, and he'd learned to play it. Nothing in particular was said about it, and Mr. Sanmartin was all unsuspecting, when one day an absurd individual who turned out to be his son's violin teacher called on him at his office and begged him to let the boy study professionally. It seemed that he had a "rare talent," and all the rest of it. Things were a bit unpleasant for a while after that. Jack had actually run out of the house when his father had broken the violin in half and thrown it in the fireplace. He'd hitch-hiked as far west as Harrisburg before they found him, and for a few months he'd been something of a problem. He scarcely spoke, and his mother went around tearfully and sniffly. Fool—giving a boy a violin. . . .

Later there had been an episode about dancing. Jack went out dancing fairly often with his friends, especially after he'd started college, and he danced well and was popular, if the number of telephone calls from girls inviting him to dancing parties indicated anything. Mr. Sanmartin had no objection to any of that. He'd known plenty of girls too, in his younger days, and as for dancing—he'd done the tango and the varsoviana all over the western hemisphere, and other steps elsewhere. But one day at breakfast Jack showed his father a card with a name and a Broadway address on it. Somebody had come up to him on a dancefloor the night before and given it to him, and told him to report the next day if he wanted to try out for a spot in a show that was rehearsing. "May I try out, Father? I won't take the job, of course, or at least we'll talk about it before I do anything, but I'd like to see if they offer it to me. May I, please?"

Mr. Sanmartin just smiled, and said "What do *you* think?"

That closed the conversation, but apparently the boy hadn't told quite the whole story. Apparently he'd given his name and number to the giver of the card, and for several days strangers kept telephoning at odd hours and asking for him. Mr. Sanmartin took some of the calls himself—Jack was forbidden to go near the telephone for a while—and was amused by the grotesque Broadway accents at the other end of the line. Jack grew more and more strained and quivering as the calls kept coming, and finally he disobeyed. He went tensely to the phone, said "Yes, this is Jack Sanmartin. Thanks a lot, but I'm definitely not interested in your proposition," and that was that. That was the kind of disobedience Mr. Sanmartin liked: it was a pleasure to see such spirit in a young man.

The boy's draft call came after his sophomore year in college, and his year in the army was Mr. Sanmartin's only period of worry. The army could be so unsettling. Would Jack come back and pick up where he'd left off? Would he not, perhaps, seize this break as an "opportunity," and go off on his own? But the army played into Mr. Sanmartin's hands. It kept Jack in southern camps, never sent him overseas, and depressed him thoroughly. He hated it. He was glad to return to the apartment and go on with college. Nowadays he still went out dancing from time to time, but the new element in his life was poetry. He'd brought back quite a number of books of poetry with him from the army—apparently he'd spent most of his spare time reading them. Now they were strewn around the house. Poetry in English, Spanish, French, Italian, even Latin—all the languages that Jack had picked up here and there throughout his life. Mr. Sanmartin dipped into some of them. Beautiful. Mr. Sanmartin was not at all insensitive to the beauties of language. But somehow in the presence of all those books his nose twitched and he smiled to himself. . . .

He had to smile openly, six weeks or so after the beginning of Jack's senior year, when the boy told him he'd invited his Latin teacher to dinner. "Latin teacher? What Latin teacher? You're not taking a Latin course, are you?" Mr. Sanmartin was always au courant with Jack's studies: he was liberal about them, too, letting him stay a full four years in college, when two or three would have been sufficient before entering Mines.

"No, I'm not taking a Latin course, but I'm visiting one."

"Visiting? Oh yes." An amusing concept, visiting a Latin course. "Visiting—I see."

"Professor Kelly's a very agreeable fellow, Father. I'd like you to meet him. He's only a few years older than I am."

"Certainly I'll meet him. With great pleasure. Ask him to dinner by all means."

Mr. Sanmartin turned his head away to hide his second smile. Something was up again! Poetry and a Latin teacher! Well, it showed that Jack was logical—in one groove, so to speak—like his father. Violin, dancing, poetry: they were all of a kind. It wasn't as though Jack were willing to seize on anything at all that wasn't mining; his rebellions were all similarly inspired. Mr. Sanmartin wasn't sorry that a new flare-up was coming. Since his return from the army Jack had been too quiet. It was time for another display of his spirit—that spirit which sooner or later, quite soon now, would make him as successful a mining engineer as his father had been.

Yes, Jack resembled him even in his high-spirited rebelliousness. Hadn't Mr. Sanmartin had to defy his own father, as a young man, in order to make for himself this career he was now passing on to Jack? The old fellow had been a bookkeeper in a Havana cigar factory all his life, and had done his best to get his son to be a bookkeeper too. Such a sure, respectable calling. He'd been indignant when the boy broke loose and went his own way, grubbing in the ground like a workman all over the world. It had had to be rather ruthless, that break with his father in Havana. But who in the world wanted to be a bookkeeper?

Mr. Sanmartin wondered, after Professor Kelly had

been at the apartment for dinner, just what wording Jack was going to use, in the approach he was so obviously planning. "Father—I don't blame you for opposing those other things that came up. They weren't the sort of things any father would want his son to go in for. I see that now. But a university . . . Latin poetry . . . Vergil . . ." Wouldn't it probably be something like that? Smiling to himself, Mr. Sanmartin thought it probably would be.

How thoroughly Mr. Sanmartin enjoyed, therefore, the news about Professor Kelly in the papers!

CHAPTER TEN

It's natural to be disappointed, isn't it, when someone who is supposed to bring good luck gives every indication not only of *not* bringing it, but of bringing bad luck instead? Especially when one takes a serious view of good-luck symbols—and Iris was a firm believer in all the little totems and tabus that theatre and near-theatre people regard, or pretend to regard, with such reverence: the whistling in the dressing rooms, the passing on stairs, and all the rest of it. To someone like that, a good-luck charm that turns out to bring bad luck is the worst kind of poison—far worse than bad luck pure and simple.

So that Iris was not only disappointed in Terence, but as eager to keep out of that once-pleasant-seeming young man's way as most of us are to shun what looks like sugar but turns out to be potassium cyanide.

Back at the time of Iris's divorce it had been Cynthia

who suggested poverty. "Don't let Penn pay you a nickel," she said. "Think of the ammunition you'll take away from the family if you refuse alimony. If you're right—if Penn's going to miss you and long for you—think what it will do to him to know you're poor. He'll eat his heart out. We'll find some way of letting him know how really poor you are."

So Iris had renounced any alimony or financial settlement and moved into furnished rooms.

And it was also Cynthia—certainly an invaluable friend—who had thought of the Latin lessons. At least, it had been her idea that The Three should take a course in something with a tutor.

This plan hadn't been adopted without some discussion. There had been objections—that it would be a bore even to have to pretend to study, and, more seriously, that the plan was corny. Cynthia admitted the latter—pointed it out, even, for she was no less a realist than the others. "But frankly, with no offense intended," she said, "I don't think it's too corny for Penn."

Iris had flushed a bit at that, and Liz, with whom Cynthia had rehearsed the conversation the day before, quickly said, "I'm sure Iris agrees with you, Cynthia, but Penn's so terribly sweet let's put it on the record. Let's say the plan probably isn't too corny for 'a sweet fellow like Penn.' Isn't it all right that way, Iris?"

Iris said it was.

Cynthia hadn't been thinking of any particular field of knowledge when she first proposed the study plan: the thing in her mind was a man—some young man of scholarly and yet attractive appearance who could be introduced as Professor So-and-so to anyone that Iris might happen to meet when she was with him. An advantageous escort, in short: one in whose company Iris wouldn't have to worry about running into any stray

Penn-Gillises or their friends or acquaintances. "'The company she keeps,' you know," Cynthia quoted, significantly. Since The Three were limited in their ideas of academic matters, Latin and Greek were the subjects that occurred to them. There was a tossup, Latin won, and the university sent Terence down in reply to Cynthia's telephone call.

It was thus scarcely an accident that Terence had been hired to give Latin lessons to The Three, except that his immediate suitability was accidental. They had expected that a long series of interviews and rejections would be necessary, that they would have to speak tactfully to the university about appearance requirements. The phenomenally rapid success of their quest contributed greatly to the confidence that all of them, but especially Iris, placed in Terence.

So that "imaginable" is the word to describe Iris's feelings when she learned from the others on Tuesday morning about the police questioning in the Grizzly Bar, and later when she read the Tuesday afternoon headlines.

Even more imaginable were her feelings when she read one of the Wednesday evening papers—a paper that came her way just after Liz had telephoned so indignantly about Terence's selfishness and conceit. Over the caption "Prof in Glad Rags, with Friend, Few Hours Before Arrest," the front page bore a photograph not only of Terence but of herself with him, snapped during one of the intermissions of *Rigoletto*. Against a background of dim figures she was smiling radiantly straight at the camera, holding a glass of champagne. It was one of the best snapshots ever taken, she realized through her stunned and horrified tears. She was magnificently recognizable—to Penn, to the Penn-Gillises, to everyone. "I'll kill him," she was shrieking by the time she got Liz on the telephone. "Kill him, kill him, torture him. . . ."

"Give me ten minutes," Liz begged. "I'll be with you in ten minutes." Liz hung up and quickly telephoned Cynthia, and Cynthia immediately telephoned Iris and kept her on the wire until Liz arrived at Iris's and heard her shouting into the receiver: "I'll kill him, I'll kill the ———— ———— ————."

Liz could see that Iris was too busy shrieking to be taking in a word of the important, just-received news that Cynthia was trying to tell her—news that Cynthia had already briefly given Liz in their mere snatch of conversation. Liz pulled the phone out of Iris's hands and said to Cynthia "I'll tell the story to Iris—you get dressed and come over."

It was a short story: Penn was coming to New York. The news had just been telephoned to Zug from Aiken by the operative whom Zug out of the goodness of his heart was paying to spend his time hanging around the Penn-Gillis service entrance, telling the maids and stable boys about Iris's poverty and broken heart and picking up what gossip he could. There'd been a violent quarrel of some kind among the Penn-Gillises, he reported, and Penn was flying to New York "quite soon" —he didn't know just when or why.

Iris's tears and sobs redoubled when Liz forced her to listen to the news. "I know why he's coming to New York," she sobbed. "To point the finger of scorn at me. To tell me that his family was right all along, that I'm only fit to associate with criminals. He's right, too. He's right—I'm just a tramp, a ————ing ————ing tramp. . . ."

By this time Cynthia had rushed across town in a cab and was with them, and she and Liz both had their arms around Iris, soothing her as best they could and assuring her that she wasn't a tramp at all. "Stop, dear," Cynthia ordered, finally. "Stop bawling this minute. Your brain'll go to pieces if you don't. It's started to go to pieces already, I'm afraid. Because you're so obviously wrong. Wrong on one thing, at least. Listen: The operative said Penn had a fight with his family down there. A *fight*. So of course you're wrong. I don't know any more than you do why he's coming north, but since he's fought with his family you can be sure it's not to tell you he *agrees* with them. Let's think, dear, think. . . ."

"In any case," sobbed Iris, "he's arriving here just in time to see this picture of me and that dirty ————ing goon. . . ."

Cynthia was frowning, her head was bowed, and she was holding all ten of her fingers to her forehead. Liz was looking at her expectantly. How hard she was thinking! Even Iris felt it, and her sobbing gave way to a silent suspense. "Indifference!" Cynthia suddenly pronounced, oracularly. "Indifference! Of course that's corny too, but as I've said before, in my opinion nothing's too corny for P. . . ."

". . . for a sweet fellow like Penn," Liz quickly amended.

"Anyway, 'Indifference!'" said Cynthia again. "It's a kind of watchword. Listen, something's bringing Penn to New York. What is it? What can it be?"

"Smart girls," she said, when the others made no answer. "Only a fool would express an opinion, with as little to go on as we have. So since you can't know why he's coming, Iris, take my advice and pretend not to care. The big thing is that he's coming. That's what we were working for, wasn't it, to get him up here? And remember the old saying—what works at a distance doesn't work close at hand. No more poverty, Iris. Penn may be eating his heart out *thinking* of you as poor, but take it from me he won't want to *see* you that way. And no more broken-hearted behavior, either. Remember the night he fell for you? You were wearing leopard-spotted satin, if I recall. And not looking poor or broken-hearted, exactly. So . . ."

Cynthia paused. "I was able to do a favor the other day," she then said, keeping her eyes directed away from the others and using a different voice, as though she were beginning quite a new conversation. "A favor for one of the most important figures in the entertainment industry. Now . . ."

Under ordinary circumstances, Iris and Liz would have behaved, following Cynthia's words, like the ladies they were. A confidence of that nature from any one of them was always an occasion for the display of impeccable manners on the part of the others. But today the emotional strain had been too great: the temptation to seek relief was irresistable. First Liz's involuntary smile broadened, and then Iris's, and soon they were laughing helplessly. "*Well*," said Cynthia, indignantly, "I *must* say . . ." But the laughter was infectious, and before long Cynthia herself was smiling, and looking only a little ruffled.

"Well," she said, "after all, girls, let's face it. Do I know who Zugie may catch sight of tomorrow, someplace? For all I know maybe he's caught sight of her today. We all know the rest of the story, once it begins. He's gorgeously generous about arrangements as you both know, but even so a girl likes to feel she's still got her own feet to stand on. So when I had a chance to do this favor for this important person in my old line . . . Well, be honest: would *you* turn down a sort of free insurance policy?"

"Sort of free!" cried Iris, with delight. "Sort of free!" And Liz merrily echoed, "*Gratuito assai! Prezioso!*"

Cynthia lowered her eyes. "Let's get back to the

point," she urged, when the hilarity had died down a little. "Because the point is that at this very minute the entertainment person in question is putting on a show. And being in the position that I'm in just now, I'm pretty sure that just by lifting that telephone I could get a friend of mine into it, provided she looks as good as you do, Iris. Just what kind of a spot he'd give you I can't say—that might depend on you a little. He's an absolutely discreet person, a very great gentleman. But anyway, whatever spot you got out of him you'd be up there behind the footlights looking beautiful and on top of the world, and if Penn fell for you at a party of Cesi's I think it's likely that if he's going to fall for you again at all . . ."

"You darling!" cried Iris. "You absolute sweetheart. . . ."

"My dear," said Cynthia, deprecatingly, "you know you'd do the same for me. But now you'd better let me telephone. The opening's only a few days off."

By the time she climbed into bed that night, or rather the next morning, Iris was pretty well tired out. Why shouldn't she have been? Following immediately after the afternoon's emotional storm as it did, the coming-to-terms at the theatre—or more precisely in the very great gentleman's private office in the theatre—hadn't been easy. He'd shown himself no mean bargainer during the hours she'd spent with him after his secretary had gone home.

And then she'd been busy with Jack Sanmartin. Jack had sounded quite breathless with pleasure when she called him about ten and suggested that they go dancing, and in no time at all he was ringing her doorbell. "This is too good to be true," he said gratefully. "I hadn't quite got my courage up yet, to call you. It's especially wonderful coming tonight. If you knew what I've been going through at home. . . ." He took her to a little place with a good Brazilian band.

In addition to his dancing there was something else about Jack that pleased Iris that night: the way he felt about Terence. As they were leaving her flat the telephone rang and rang and rang—not the first time it had gone unanswered since Terence had been in the papers. Jack stared at her questioningly, and when she said "I imagine it's you know who, and I'm not having any," he nodded in sympathy. "I don't mind telling you," he said, "that Professor Kelly has let me down in a big way, getting mixed up in all this."

"Me too," said Iris. "What's he done to you?"

Jack told her a little. "Now Father brings up my 'respectable friend the professor,' in every second sentence," he said. "Damn everything anyway. I don't much care what I do. To hell with Father and the professor and everybody. *Almost* everybody, that is. Now tell me about *you* and the professor."

"If you don't mind," said Iris, "I won't. For personal reasons that we won't go into I feel I'm going off my nut whenever I hear his name."

"I'd a million times rather talk about you anyway," Jack said. And as they rolled around the room in a samba he told her how crazy he'd been about her ever since seeing her in the Vergil seminar.

"Tell me," Iris said, after murmuring how sweet he was, "have you ever thought of dancing professionally, instead of just socially like this?"

And when he told her that he'd not only thought of it, but was in a mood to begin doing it at a moment's notice, she smiled happily. "I need just the right partner for a good spot I've been promised in a show that's opening in a few days," she said. "You dance so divinely, and you're so nice and dark and I'm so blonde and we look so interesting together, I wonder if you'd consider coming around to the theatre now? I happen to know there's a rehearsal going on. . . ."

Just before closing time that night, between two of her last numbers, Myra was called to the Grizzly Bar telephone.

"The moral of the story is, nothing succeeds like success," Max said jauntily. "This Jack and Iris team happened to dance to your minuet Monday night and were nuts about it. The show they're in opens *next* Monday —you'll rehearse beginning tomorrow. The act's a rumble or a samble or something, but they want to make it a novelty: they won't hear of doing it to anything but a harpsichord played by you. You can make it easy— it's between dinner music and the bar. Street traffic's nothing, during theatre hours."

Myra told him to sign her up. She smiled to herself as she left the phone. Today she'd been feeling better than she'd felt for some time. She'd have liked to think it was because she was getting used to everything between herself and Terence being definitely over. But it was probably because Terence was out of jail and out of his mess. Yes—she was afraid it was probably that. She smiled with happiness whenever she thought of it. When she'd read about Terence's predicament in the Tuesday papers she'd been half crazy with worry, and then when she'd seen him at his aunt's, a free man, she'd been so relieved that it took all her pride to keep from showing it.

CHAPTER ELEVEN

After his visit to the Medical Center Terence stopped at the library and at Ramsay's, collected books and photographs, and had them called for by Western Union for delivery. Then, early Thursday morning, after a restless night, he went to the office of Mr. Krebs, an attorney formerly associated with his father. Terence could remember from his boyhood that his father had not esteemed Krebs, and had been speaking at the time of his death about breaking the partnership. This had set off one of the numerous disagreements that he could remember taking place between his parents: his mother had defended Krebs because he was "such a gentleman," and after his father's death it was by Mr. Krebs that she allowed affairs relating to the estate to be handled. Terence had consulted him after his return from overseas, and now he turned to him naturally following the defection of Slade and Slade and his own inability to extract an alibi from Ramsay.

The attorney, old-school in appearance to the point of wearing a collar which of course was not, but seemed to be, made of celluloid, greeted him with patriarchal expressions of affection, and, when he had heard his story, placed a hand on his knee. "I am glad you have come to me in this dilemma," he said. "But you must think of me as being what I am, an old family friend, rather than as merely a lawyer, and you must unburden yourself to me as you would have to your dear father. As man to man, dear fellow, what was there between this milliner woman and yourself?"

Terence went over his story once again, speaking very distinctly and emphatically, and with obvious disappointment Mr. Krebs seemed finally to accept it. "Pshaw, my boy," he said, "if that's all there is to it what are you worried about? You may be indicted, of course, but that doesn't mean you'll go to the chair. Scarcely a chance of that. A very negligible percentage of error occurs in the house."

"The house?"

"The death house. I'm convinced that very few people are sent there, or from there to the chair, by error. Very few indeed."

"If it could be arranged," said Terence hastily, "I'd much prefer to avoid even indictment. Wouldn't that be possible?"

Mr. Krebs lifted his hands. "As a layman you'd be astonished to learn how many good men have been indicted for murder at one time or another in their lives. Indictment proves nothing, except that a grand jury of twenty-three citizens agrees that reasonable cause exists to hold you in connection with a crime. I assure you, my dear boy, that were you indicted my high opinion of you wouldn't be altered in the slightest. So you see it's really a minor matter."

"But the publicity . . ."

"Ah yes. The university public relations officer was displeased, I think you said, and you yourself did not enjoy it. So our desired goal might be stated thusly: avoidance of indictment because of inevitable publicity resulting therefrom?"

Terence nodded.

"And this desired goal is to be attained in the absence of an alibi?"

"It is."

"I'm afraid it is not," corrected Mr. Krebs, gently.

"People without alibis are strawberries and cream to grand juries: they smack their lips over them. Get your alibi, Terence, and the indictment business will take care of itself."

Terence's heart sank, but the attorney had a suggestion as to how the alibi might, after all, be obtained. "Visit your friend again," he said, "and this time take along someone from headquarters to witness your conversation. The presence of a police detective has been known to jog the stubbornest memory. And if on the other hand your friend persists in pretending forgetfulness, an officer trained in such matters will probably spot significant inconsistencies in his story. If it's satisfactory to you I'll just ring the Inspector now and get him to arrange for one of his people to meet you at the Medical Center. What time do you want to go?"

After telephoning to the university physician and then to the floor nurse Terence made his appointment for the afternoon, and Mr. Krebs talked with the Inspector. "Most satisfactory," he pronounced, when he hung up. "He is delighted to cooperate. You know, I understand the Inspector's position perfectly, and I think that you should too, Terence, despite its unpleasantness for you. Considering the absence of an alibi, and the fact that, as he says the woman mentioned you practically with her dying breath, the poor fellow would be remiss in his duty if he didn't press for an indictment. He was awfully apologetic. Said he'd instruct his man to keep his ears wide open this afternoon and pay strict attention to everything your friend has to say."

That was all that Mr. Krebs could think of for the moment. "Let me know what happens up there," he said, "and we'll go on from that point. Don't worry. Above all, don't worry about the house."

"The house? Oh, yes . . ."

Terence hurried back to the university.

He had a different set of classes from those of the previous day: once again there were requests for autographs. At lunchtime he avoided the Club and bought a delicatessen sandwich to eat in his flat. Then he tried to sleep away the time before his appointment. But the attempt was a failure, and in his restlessness he read the morning newspaper—in which for a change there was no mention of him—from front to back, even to the ads.

The flat was a dreary little place—a good deal drearier, especially by daylight, than he had realized while acquiring it. Books were its chief furnishing, but books of forbidding aspect: shelves full of works on quantum mechanics, and numerous other volumes bearing titles of which *The Elementary Physical Particles and Their Interactions* was among the most frivolous. There were rows of bound numbers of *The Physical Review,* and an entire shelf given over to something mysteriously called *Det Kgl. Danske Videnskabernes Selskab—Mathematisk, Fysiske, Meddelelser.* Not the most suitable atmosphere for a love-nest, exactly: it was more redolent of dissolution than of dissoluteness, so to speak. Anything less venereal—for a humanist, at least—could scarcely be imagined: all too fitting that he had not been able to put the place to its intended use! Certainly there seemed little chance of that now: the repeated non-answering of Iris's telephone and the cold voices of the di Cesare and Zug butlers telling him that their mistresses were out had left him without illusion as to the state of the weather in those quarters.

The gentleman from headquarters who was awaiting him in the corridor outside Ramsay's room when he arrived at the Medical Center was not one of those who had so astonished him by calling at his flat on Tuesday morning to escort him downtown, but he closely resembled them. "Good afternoon, Professor," he said touching his fedora. "McSweeny, attached to headquarters. Are we all set for the new try? Remember now," he advised, "when we go in the thing for you to do is to get Mr. Ramsay talking and to *keep* him talking. You never can tell when he may slip up on some revealing detail, no matter how carefully he watches himself."

"As a trained observer," Terence asked, "is there any particular approach that you recommend?"

"The subject of yourself is the one he's most likely to be helpful about. So keep as close to that as you can, I'd say. All set?"

And having received a nod of approval from the floor nurse at her station down the hall they entered the room with the barred windows.

Today poor Ramsay had an air that was almost childlike, sitting up as he was in bed amid a litter of books, papers and photographs: he was like an elderly little boy with the measles, propped up among his playthings. "Oh, so there you are, Terence," he said, a bit abstractedly, looking up from one of his volumes. "I don't mind telling you I'm pretty close to despair."

"I'm sorry to hear it, Ramsay. This is Mr. McSweeny."

Ramsay gave no indication of having heard. "Pretty close to despair," he repeated, shaking his head. "Here I've spent the entire day poring over Peter Lombard, one of the greatest Church Fathers of all, and what do I find? Exactly the same sentences about the mousetrap that we found in Gersonius. *Exactly!* And whereas Gersonius had the decency to say they came from Augustine, Peter Lombard has the gall to pass them off without any attribution, as though they were his own. Can you imagine? One Church Father stealing from another?

Can you think of anything more disillusioning? Or anything less helpful to a poor scholar like myself, interested only in discovering the truth?"

"Listen, Ramsay. The truth is what I'm interested in, too, at the moment. One truth especially. But before we begin, this is Mr. McSweeny, from Police Headquarters. Won't you shake hands with him?"

For a moment Ramsay's gaze darted uncertainly between his two visitors, like the glances of a bird in the presence of humans, and then he inclined his head. "How do you do, Mr. McSweeny. Very pleased to have you with us. I trust you may find the seminar enjoyable. Of course there's no lack of discussion of Joseph's role in the writings of the Fathers," he went on with scarcely a pause. "There's endless justification of the relationship between him and Mary, for example—to show that it is a true marriage despite the perpetual virginity of the couple, and so forth. But as far as mousetraps are concerned . . ."

"Tell me one thing, Ramsay," Terence interrupted resolutely. "Do you remember last Wednesday, the night of my birthday, when you first showed me the Joseph triptych? You said . . ."

Ramsay's voice was suddenly cool. "If you will allow me to continue with the seminar, Terence . . ."

"You do remember it was Wednesday that you showed me the triptych, don't you, Ramsay? You remember my asking you to let me spend my birthday evening with you, don't you?"

"I remember many things about you, Terence. I can assure you of that. But I prefer to discuss more interesting subjects just now. If you insist on interrupting again, I . . ."

"Ramsay, do me the favor of getting away from *Muscipula Diaboli* just for a minute. We'll come right back to it. But just now I find myself in a situation . . ."

"Another situation like the one in Paris, perhaps? A love affair with a cocotte that looks like your mother?"

Terence flushed and winced. But he went bravely ahead. This was what McSweeny had advised as most useful, wasn't it? A discussion of the subject of himself? "She didn't *look* like my mother, Ramsay. It was just that her figure . . ."

"Forgive me if I indulge in what seems to be an inescapable and sordid parenthesis, Mr. McSweeny. I'll make it as short as possible. Tell me, Terence: are the details of your new situation, whatever it is, just as elevating as the Paris details? The seduction in the hotel bedroom? The week or two of amorous madness? The celebration with the lady wearing your mother's dress? And then, almost immediately, the death of your mother. . . . You were so naive about it all. You seemed to think it so personal a situation. So entirely your own. Whereas actually it's classical, a sort of classical case history. A first affair, rather overdue, made possible by a girl's resemblance in some way to one's mother. Then the mother's death, followed by feelings of guilt that kill the affair and make future affairs difficult or impossible. Do you think some of the rest of us haven't been through such things, Terence—through the same situation, up to one point or another? There are variations, of course. The mother can be just as powerful alive as dead. Some of us know that. There's nothing unique about your story, Terence, much as your conceit makes you want to think so."

Terence felt himself quite crimson.

"But *when* was it that I told you all this, Ramsay?" he asked hopefully. "What day of the week?"

"Now, now—you know perfectly well what day of the week it was. . . ."

In the acuteness of his embarrassment Terence had been avoiding Mr. McSweeny's eye, but now he saw that the policeman was, unseen by Ramsay, making notes under the cover of his hat, which was perched on his knees. He caught Terence's eye and gave an encouraging nod. Had he learned something useful, then? Had Ramsay said something significant? How upsetting to think that he had been absorbing all these details that Wednesday night, while seeming so absent in mind! The words "absence" and "presence" certainly took on new meanings as far as Ramsay's mind was concerned today, poor fellow. At the moment he no longer seemed childish, sitting in his bed among his books and papers, but most unlike himself in another way—positively passionate and denunciatory. He gave the impression of seeing things in his own past and hating the sight of them.

"All that whining about your childhood! As though it was any different from the childhood of any of the rest of us! Those of us with mothers like yours, I mean. A mother that wore the pants, had her own way, even had the luck—*she* considered it luck—to be able to bring you up all by herself. It didn't take her long, after your father's death, to switch you away from the law to something she thought more refined or something, did it? *I* know all about those things. *I* know who it usually is that gets a boy's nerves upset and shunts him into some precious by-path. I recognized your story the minute I heard it. I was able to fill in the outlines without half trying. . . ."

McSweeny was still making notes. He looked pleased, and once again nodded encouragingly as Terence cast him a pitiable glance.

But suddenly it became clear that Ramsay had finished. Even more suddenly than he had begun his tirade, he ended it, moving back into his seminar with the briefest of transitions. "I hope you're satisfied, Terence," he said. "Satisfied with the amount of valuable classroom time I've given up to discussion of your affairs. You've been most egotistically exigent today. It's not like you. I will not be deflected again, I warn you. Where were we? Oh yes—the Joseph legend. . . ."

And until the arrival of the nurse to say that his visitors had overstayed their time, Ramsay gave his students a lengthy and inexorable dissertation on Joseph—with particular emphasis on his age at his death, and comments on its theological significance drawn from the writings of Saints Bernard, Bonaventura, Thomas and others.

He was graciousness itself by the time they left. "It's not your fault that I haven't found any more than I have in all these books, Terence," he said. "Thanks again for sending them. I'll keep trying. Why *does* that mousetrap disappear? Why? Why?" And to Mr. McSweeny he extended the wish that on some future occasion he might again feel like attending the seminar. "Come and see me soon, Terence," were his parting words. "I'm apparently to be here indefinitely."

Both Terence's natural eagerness to ask McSweeny about the outcome of the experiment, which had been so much more grueling than he had expected, and his involuntary speculation as to what confused concept of "here" might at the moment be in poor Ramsay's mind, were interrupted by the lightning-like disappearance of the man from headquarters the moment they left the room. He rushed off flinging the word 'telephone' over his shoulder, and Terence waited for him rather lengthily in the hall. "I just made my report to the Chief," he said when he returned, "and he thinks the best thing would be for you or your lawyer to get in touch with headquarters in the morning. I got a lot of interesting stuff—but it's his orders that that's about all I can tell you."

"Everything's all right, then?"

"Oh, everything's fine, fine. . . ."

Terence telephoned Mr. Krebs as soon as he reached home. "Capital, capital," the attorney said. "I'll give our friend the Inspector a buzz in the morning. In the meanwhile, relax, my boy. You're in good hands, if I say so myself. Have a good time of some kind tonight. Some *divertissement* to relieve the strain. 'Music hath charms,' you know. Terpsichore was the muse I adored at your age."

In the lamplight the atomist's flat looked a little less dreary than it had looked at noon, and Terence began to feel some hope that the news of his exoneration, which would be appearing in the papers in twenty-four hours, might result, with a little patience, in proper use of the place after all.

"Here," said Miss Quinn scornfully a little later, when he had made himself comfortable in her kitchen, "this will give you a chance to see for yourself just how broadminded your Aunt May Mahony is."

Terence took the letter she offered him. In it May revealed that Mount St. Margaret's had indeed notified the Massachusetts relatives of Miss Quinn's application for admission, and she described the nature of their joint reply, composed by herself. She was sorry to have to say, she wrote, that they had felt morally obliged to suggest that the Reverend Mother make sure that Miss Quinn had received absolution for "a certain episode in her private life."

"I don't sense much sorrow, do you?" Miss Quinn asked Terence. "The whole thing reminds me of the

Scribes and the Pharisees and the woman taken in adultery. I guess they're all scared I might do something scandalous at Mount St. Margaret's—something that would make Mahony lose his undertaking business or get poor Vincent unfrocked."

She was in surprisingly good spirits for someone whose family had just sabotaged her plans for a peaceful old age: the opportunity to think of herself as a Gospel heroine seemed to be a fairly satisfactory substitute. "Of course I've given up all thought of Mount St. Margaret's, even if they accept me," she said. "I wouldn't dream of going there under this cloud. Don't you think I might have got tired of a purely women's Home, anyway? But there aren't many co-ed places, and I understand they're mostly restricted to stage people or Mooses or Elks. . . ."

Pleased by his visit, she chattered on about all kinds of things as she got dinner ready and set their places. She presumed a bit, eventually. "If only you and Myra would be friends again and come back here with me I think I'd stay on after all, just to show my dear relations I can still paddle my own canoe. But as it is . . ."

As a pretext for changing the conversation Terence seized on the first thing he caught sight of—a photograph standing on the kitchen cupboard. "Who's that nice-looking fellow, Auntie? Haven't I seen his face someplace before?"

And it became instantly apparent that Miss Quinn's good spirits following the receipt of her sister's letter had been surface good spirits only, for those few words of Terence's destroyed them. "You've *forgotten* Gus?" she cried, with instant tears. "He's not only gone but *forgotten?*"

It was too big a mistake to remedy with mere words.

Terence went hurriedly over to his aunt and put a penitent arm around her shaking shoulders.

"Forgotten what Gus looked like, after only seven short years! Such a good man. . . ."

"Of course he was a good man, Auntie. Of course I hadn't forgotten what he looked like. It's just that you hadn't had his picture out for so long." Terence thought wistfully of Mr. Krebs's prescription of a good time.

"I came across it this morning, sorting things over upstairs. Just having him there on the kitchen-cupboard all day made me feel better than I thought I'd ever feel again after getting that letter from May. What a family I have! When I think of how your own mother, the sister I'd always been closest to, acted about Gus. . . . Hasn't he the sweetest face? Remember those clever pickle advertisements his company used to run in the *Pickle Gazette*? Remember how proud he was of them? How he used to cut them out and paste them in his scrapbook? He took the scrapbook with him, you know: he'd never be separated from that. Or his music. All he took with him was just his clothes and his pickle scrapbook and his flute and his radio. . . ." Miss Quinn dabbed at her red eyes.

Terence well remembered Gus's flute and radio. He remembered his technique on the one, and the type of musical program to which he had usually dialed the other, and especially he remembered Gus's fondness for playing the flute as an accompaniment to radio melodies.

"I'd give anything to hear a nice flute obbligato again. All today with Gus's picture there I kept the music programs turned on hoping for one, but no luck. Just a lot of symphonies. . . ."

Once again Terence thought of Mr. Krebs, and something stirred in his recent memory. "Could I see a newspaper, Aunt Kitty? I'd like to glance at the music page. How about coming out with me and hearing something nice? If I find something, that is. Yes—here we are. . . ."

CHAPTER TWELVE

It hadn't taken Sadie very long to get over any serious wish that Joe might get his hands on the professor or that she herself might scratch the professor's eyes out. But Joe was brooding and restless during the days following his release. Try as he might, he said, he couldn't put the professor out of his mind. "How *can* I forget that lousy story of his?" he demanded when Sadie urged him to do just that. "He shouldn't be allowed to get away with it. Why, if you happened to be different that story could have knocked hell out of both our lives."

"But I'm not different, so the story doesn't hurt us at all, so try to think of something pleasant."

"I can't. I keep coming back to it. I've got to see him and punch him in the nose. . . ."

Sadie let him know what she'd come to think of that idea.

"Besides, I want to ask him just what the milliner said when she told him I was expected. I keep feeling that hanging over me, honey, my being expected that night. If the professor could tell me just what words she used, maybe it would clear up . . ."

The Legal Aid Society lawyer, consulted by telephone, advised strongly against approaching the professor or anybody else. "Don't go looking for trouble," he said. "If any steps are to be taken, let other people take them. Sit tight. You're in a good safe seat, in my opinion."

But the professor's two stories preyed on Joe's mind and made it hard for him to work. He taught his morning settlement house classes, but afternoons he kept walking away from his glue pots and his press and looking out the window. "Wish you could take a walk," he said, the second afternoon, when he saw Sadie looking at him. "A walk would do me good, but not alone."

"No walking for me. I'll sit in the park with you, though, if you like."

They took a bus to the park and sat in the zoo and watched the animals and the humans—the babies and mothers and nurses, the lovers and old people, and the popcorn sellers and balloon sellers. Joe put his arm around her and bought some popcorn. "A week or two from now we won't be coming to the park," he said. "A year from now we'll be buying balloons."

"She'll—he'll—be pretty small for balloons by then, won't he—she?"

"Think so? Look at that one. He—she's—enjoying it."

The small occupant of a baby-carriage was staring fixedly at a yellow balloon that a big red-headed balloon seller was tying to the handle-bars. Sadie laughed. "Enjoying? Just a big stare meaning a big blur where the mind may be some day."

"Ours has a mind already. I can feel it tick right now, under my hand."

"Kick, you mean."

The red-headed balloon-seller was still tying the yellow balloon to the baby-carriage, or rather, he was still trying to. "Not born yet," said Joe, "but more of a mind already than that redhead. Look at him. Shall I tell him to take his gloves off?"

"Mind your business. What did the lawyer say about not looking for trouble?"

"He was talking about professors, not balloon-sellers. Can't I just say 'Why not try taking your gloves off, you dumb bunny?' He'd just hit me, and I'd hit him, and we'd have some fun. He's big, but he looks kinda pooped. Probably harmless."

"Tease me all you want to, when you're happy."

"I am teasing you and I am happy."

"Won't you try and stay so, please?"

When the sun began to sink behind the buildings on Central Park West they got up to go. "Now to the workbench," said Joe, "since I took the afternoon off. Got to earn balloon money for next year, you know."

"You won't have much time to work today. If it didn't cost so much, I'd say let's stay uptown and eat, instead of going all the way down and coming right back again. But I've got the rest of that stew from last night in the icebox. . . ."

"Are you telling me something? Are we going someplace tonight?"

"Just a little surprise I went out and bought this morning. Kind of a cheering-up surprise. I thought you needed it. Especially since . . ."

"Yes?"

". . . I'd like it too."

She showed him the tickets. "Not very good seats. They never are at this price when you buy them at the last minute. We won't see much. But I think we're almost directly over the violins. . . ."

CHAPTER THIRTEEN

All was anticipation at the Zug dinner-table. Or, more accurately, The Three were anticipatory—everything was so promising. The men, as usual in this early, comparatively unstimulated part of the evening, were still on the repressed side, out of the spirit of things, tending to mull over the day's business. "That *puttana Cubana* bought the *credenza*," Cesi mentioned gloomily to Liz, breaking into the gossip for a moment. "But not the Venetian sofa. She said it had too many legs. As if a Venetian sofa could!"

"The more everything the better on anything Venetian, *caro*," Liz said soothingly. "Everybody knows that."

"Everybody except that *miseraccia*." Cesi hissed the epithet at his customer, seeming to locate her somewhere in his shrimps. "*Miseraccia!*"

And Zug, too, although dressed for the Opera like everybody else, had not yet psychologically left his office. "The dirty swindler," he muttered, in a kind of trance, obviously not referring to any of his guests but to someone unhappily encountered during the day. "When I think that last year I was in a position to throw him to the dogs and didn't. . . ."

The ladies were untroubled by these particles of business-day sediment afloat in the evening wine: they would settle soon enough, they knew, and all would be clear and sparkling. How nice that a box had unexpectedly come through for tonight! Under normal conditions two operas in a week would be too many, but what with Iris's show opening on Monday . . . It was a chance for one more evening out together before—before what? Who knew *what* was ahead? That was what put them all in such high spirits: the future was full of possibilities, the way the future should be.

There hadn't been another word from the operative in Aiken. He was biding his time, apparently, until he should have definite news to give—definite news of Penn, who was probably waiting to start north until he should have absorbed a few more ounces of sunlight and strength, poor boy. After all, he had been through so much. But soon now he'd be coming, and then Iris . . .

Would Iris make the grade? She looked as though she might, certainly. Splendid was the only word. Any girl's looks would probably show the effect of moving out of furnished rooms into the Park-Yorkshire, as Iris had done. Perhaps some of her splendor was due to that. The tiger-stripe dress helped, too. They had thought of reproducing the leopard-skin satin that had been so effective the last time, but exact reproduction had seemed a little obvious, even for Penn. So Saks had put together the tiger-stripe jersey—Cynthia's suggestion—in twenty-four hours. What a success! "All you need is a slinky tail, darling!" Cynthia cried, in a combination of admiration and self-congratulation when Iris came in and took off her wrap and swept her tawny, black-striped self around the room and smiled a confident, tigerish smile. But Cynthia was mistaken. Iris didn't need a tail. She had other ornamentations, such as no tiger or even tigress had ever possessed, and which rose out of the stripes and looked all the whiter and rounder and more wonderful by contrast. It was comical, during dinner, to watch Cesi and even Zug, who after all was well acquainted with Iris's attributes. How completely, as they became more and more conscious of Iris, they snapped out of their business-day comas! "Now now," their wives teased them, as their double-takes kept increasing in violence. "Eyes front, boys! Eyes *up!*"

Her show would be chic, Iris told everybody. At least the Jack and Iris number would be. "Just a spotlight," she said, "showing darling little Drysdale at her harpsichord playing Bach or something—you know, to give her a spot of her own for a bit—and then a gradual change of rhythm until to everybody's surprise it turns into a samba, and out I come in this dress and Jack in tails and we swoosh around divinely together if I say so myself and the mike gradually makes the harpsichord louder and louder till the whole theatre's throbbing with that wonderful jungle rhythm and everybody's excited just listening and looking. . . ."

The others had barely glimpsed Jack at *Rigoletto* and in the Grizzly Bar, and they asked Iris for particulars. She described his good looks. "Dark—good for the samba. And good for another reason, too. I mean he's *really* dark—spickish—so that Penn can see there's nothing to worry about for a second. Doesn't that make it perfect? Poor Jack—he's going through his agony this very minute, I'm afraid. Telling his father about the show. There'll be hell to pay, Jack says, but he doesn't care. That's why he couldn't come to dinner. He'll join us in the box."

"I'm afraid it's only Mozart tonight," said Cynthia regretfully. "He tinkles, doesn't he? Nothing very profound, as I recall."

But the others assured her they didn't care. "It's such fun being together tonight it doesn't make any difference what we hear," said Liz. And Cynthia, expressing their feelings in the clever way she had, said, "You mean it isn't where we're going that counts—wherever we go, tonight's like a toast to the future." Everyone agreed, and looked affectionately at Iris. "A toast to the future!"

cried Zug, standing up and waving his glass. "To the future—especially Iris's!" And while they were toasting, the butler brought in a telegram and Zug opened it and gave a shout. "From Aiken," he said. "From the operative. Listen: 'Have been incapacitated twenty-four hours unable perform duties. Believe developments may have taken place will ascertain and inform.' What do you suppose that means, folks? 'Believe developments may have taken place': what do you suppose that means?"

"It could mean anything!" cried Iris, terribly agitated. "It could mean that Penn . . ."

There was a shrill note in her voice, and with only the briefest glance at Liz Cynthia quickly stood up. "Time to go, everybody," she said. "Take it easy, Iris. Remember: '*Indifference!*' Let's go now. Forget the telegram, Iris. It doesn't tell us anything. It shouldn't have been sent. *Forget it.* Come on. . . ."

But they were all more keyed up, as they piled out of the house and into the limousine, than they had expected to be.

"Flutes even in the overture!" Miss Quinn cried in delight, causing many a "Sh!" to be directed toward them in the dress-circle darkness. "Even in the overture! This is the darlingest treat!"

Terence found it a treat, too. A treat to his nerves. It probably wasn't what Mr. Krebs had had in mind when he'd suggested a good time. A 150-year-old opera designed especially to allow one's aunt to commune with the spirit of her flute-playing, legally deceased husband-except-in-the-sight-of-God is scarcely apt to be what one's lawyer means when he uses the word *divertissement*. But 'music hath charms,' and especially, for Terence, the music of Mozart had always had them; and as the overture unrolled and ended, and the curtain rose on Prince Tamino and the serpent, and the three ladies used their silver javelins and disappeared, and Papageno, clad in feathers, sang his glockenspiel song, he felt himself relaxing for the first time since the beginning of his trouble.

Yes, a notice of his exoneration in the newspapers was all that would be required to put things to rights, to get things moving again from the point at which they had stopped. The atomist's flat would bloom with all the flowers of Venus—delayed, but all the headier for the waiting. . . .

Now the three ladies—in veils, for a reason presumably known to the librettist—returned to the stage. They talked nonsense, and then next to Terence in the darkness his aunt made sounds of ecstasy as Tamino melted her heart with the picture aria; and then after applause and more nonsense came thunder and the Queen of the Night, majestic and spangled with stars.

How good it was, after all that had gone by, to live for a few hours in this fantastic, nonsensical, Mozartean world!

In the box, Cynthia apologized again. "Dreadfully tinkly," she lamented. "Like finger exercises. I'm sorry. We'll just have to make the best of it. Or if you find you simply can't stand it, let me know."

Liz shrugged in resignation, but Iris spoke sharply, "What's wrong with tinkling? I assure you when Drysdale begins to tinkle out our samba . . ."

The others nudged each other. Iris was edgy, poor thing. And who could blame her?

Of course Iris was edgy. She peered out tensely from the box as though it were possible to pick someone out of the crowd in the vast Opera House—as though there were someone there she expected to find. Was it possible that during those twenty-four hours in Aiken, while the operative had been "incapacitated," whatever that meant, Penn had without the operative's knowledge gone to an airfield and . . . ? Iris peered and wondered.

Cesi, too, was restless. From the anteroom came sounds of his displeasure—sounds of contempt directed against the language in which the opera was being performed. *"Opera non cantata in Italiano non è opera a fatto,"* he muttered. *"Barbarita! Bestia!"*

"Read your newspapers, *caro,*" Liz called back. "You can really stop listening if you just try a little." She'd had the chauffeur stop the limousine, on the way from the Zugs', and pick up an armful of newspapers for Cesi's use during the performance. This was only Thursday, and he'd given himself too thorough a manicure during *Rigoletto* on Monday to be expected to devote himself whole-heartedly to that occupation so soon again. "Just keep reading," she called, to the annoyance of people in adjoining boxes. "You'll find you won't hear a thing."

Halfway through the act Jack Sanmartin arrived. He seemed surprised, in the anteroom, to have to brush past two men immersed in newspapers—for by this time Zug as well as Cesi had taken refuge from the tinkling—but the chief expression on the boy's face was something else. "Poor thing," Iris murmured, after he'd reached the box and she'd introduced him to the others. "Was it so terrible?"

"Awful," said Jack, looking worried, almost sick. "*Awful*. And the worst thing is I'm not sure it's over. Father said something wild about coming down here. He wants to see you. He was in a terrible state when I rushed away. Perhaps I shouldn't have left him."

"Good heavens," said Iris, alarmed. "I do hope . . ."

Just then came a shout from the anteroom—a shout

from Cesi that was like the shout from Zug when he'd read the wire from Aiken. "*Ecco!*" Cesi cried. "*Guardate!*" He came hurrying into the box brandishing one of his newspapers, crackling and rattling it so that neighbors called furious protests. "Look at this!" But the light in the box was too poor to see anything by, and filled with wonder The Three and Jack hastily left their chairs and crowded back after Cesi into the anteroom. "Prof Kelly, Murder Suspect, Had Paris 'Friend,'" he read to them. "Seeking Alibi, Visits Other Prof, Who Spills All. Exclusive, by McGonigal McSweeny, Staff Writer."

"In a dramatic mental sparring contest today in an antiseptic, barred-windowed little room in the Medical Center, Professor Terence Kelly, recently held in connection with the murder of an East Side milliner, came off a bad second to an old friend and colleague from whom he was vainly seeking confirmation of the alibi he claims for the murder night. Employing smart unexpected feints, jabs and uppercuts, his opponent, Mr. Alan Ramsay, who is recovering from a recent nervous breakdown, not only successfully defended himself against his interlocutor but let spill a whole series of interesting personal revelations that took the Prof by surprise and left him still gasping on the mat when the referee reached ten. Heavenly mousetraps, Parisian love-nests and other such exotic details littered the conversation of the pundits, who . . ."

"God damn it!" cried Iris, frantically, all her stripes quivering. "Hasn't the bastard been in the papers *enough*? Isn't he satisfied? Couldn't he have the elementary decency to . . ."

Calming, gentle hands were laid upon her, and Cesi was begged to continue.

"While serving overseas with the American army, it came to light, the professor of Latin and a charming young Parisienne of the demi-monde . . . Mother-resemblance. . . . Seduction in a hotel. . . . Sudden demise. . . . Remorse. . . . 'Hands off the girls'. . . ."

From their seats in the balcony the Giulianos could, if they leaned forward far enough, catch a glimpse of one small corner of the stage. Egyptian slaves were occupying it at the moment, arranging cushions and conversing in recitative. But the Giulianos weren't watching them. They were sitting back in their seats, eyes closed, holding hands, floating away on the sounds of violins and flutes rising up like a musical cloud from the pit below. Every once in a while they looked at each other and smiled, or clasped hands more tightly.

"I could almost forget about the professor now," Joe whispered.

"Let's both forget him this minute, then. Once and for all. . . ."

The presentation of the golden flute brought more sounds of pleasure from Miss Quinn, and then, as the act neared its close and the Prince sang the aria with the omnipresent flutes—flutes in the orchestra, on the stage and in the wings—she spilled over with a little whimper. "Oh Terence darling, if only Gus were here listening too. . . ."

Terence patted her hand and gave her his handkerchief when her own became useless. And when the lights came on for the intermission he said, "Let's go out, Auntie," thinking of Mr. Krebs's advice again. "Let's go out and have a drink, by all means."

There was a crowd and a crush at the bar, but almost

at once the tiger stripes, fulfilling their function, attracted his eyes as they were attracting everybody else's. "Excuse me a minute, will you Auntie?" he said in some agitation, rather unceremoniously leaving her and her drink to shift for themselves. "Iris!" he called. "Iris!"

The entire Zug party heard him and looked his way; and then they waited for him, as he came toward them, without saying a word. There were curious half-grins on the faces of Zug and Cesi, and the expressions of The Three and of Jack Sanmartin were also somehow disquieting. "Iris," said Terence, feeling that something was queer. "I want to tell you . . ."

Quite abruptly, to his astonishment, Cesi pulled out a newspaper from his pocket and thrust it in his face. "You've seen this, I suppose?" he asked, laughing, and Zug burst into a guffaw. "Prof Kelly, Murder Suspect, Had Paris 'Friend,'" Terence saw, in a kind of daze, just a few inches from his nose; and suddenly Iris, who'd said nothing but whose eyes had been roaming all over the room, started to sob. "There's Penn!" she cried, in a kind of agony. "Over there! And oh God he sees me, and here I am with this killer!" The others stared in the direction of Iris's gaze and saw a blonde head, and one of them said "My God, it is Penn!" Terence thought that odd, for the person he saw coming toward them through the crowd was Mr. Sanmartin. But before he could solve the mystery he felt himself reeling: Iris, he dimly realized, had slapped his face, and it was burning and stinging. "Get away from me," she was shouting. "Get away and stay away, you God damned . . ."

"Indifference!" cried Cynthia, making everything seem crazier than ever, and at that moment Mr. Sanmartin reached them, wearing an alarming expression. "I wish to speak to you, madam," he said to Iris. Stiff cords were standing out unpleasantly on his neck, and his eyes were blazing. "Keep away," he ordered his son, who was remonstrating with him and begging him to "be careful." "Keep away, I warn you."

"Most unfortunate for you, madam," he said to Iris, "that you should have tried, and tried successfully, to swerve *this* boy, of all the boys in the world, from the path that someone wiser than you had chosen for him. I am sorry for you, madam, but it was many years ago that I decided what the penalty would be for anyone who should succeed in doing what you have done."

He seemed quite crazy, Mr. Sanmartin, and one of his hands was in his pocket. And then, glancing about at the mesmerized group with his blazing eyes, he suddenly caught sight of Terence; and he started, and smiled, and seemed to relax. "Forget what I just said, madam," he went on, apparently still speaking to Iris but turning a bit and staring and smiling now straight at Terence. "You were but an instrument, placed in my boy's hands by this great scholar and gentleman. He introduced my boy to you, I understand. The Latin trap did not succeed, but the dancing, this show I have been hearing about, is his responsibility. I am pleased to be able to address myself to him directly, madam, rather than to you, with whom I was resigned, not entirely happily, to have my accounting *faute de mieux*. . . ."

And then Mr. Sanmartin gave a grimace, and his hand moved in his pocket, and there was an explosion, and something gave Terence's shoulder a push that was a thousand times harder than Iris's slap, and he fell to the floor.

"Indifference!" he heard Cynthia say again, amid the screaming in English, Italian and other languages that broke out all around them. "Indifference, remember! Let's get the hell out of here. Come on—out fast, everybody!" And the Zug party almost instantly disappeared, vanishing into what seemed to be a general stampede, and for a time that was all Terence knew.

When he revived, the room seemed to be empty except for a cluster of people immediately around him, and there was a pain in his shoulder. Looking up he caught a glimpse of his aunt, her face puckered and bewildered. "A baby's being born in the Powder Room," he thought he heard somebody say. "Somebody's got caught in the crush and the baby started to come and it's almost here by now. See the husband standing there outside the door? That tall fellow looking upset? The doctor's inside—came just in time; he'll be here for this fellow on the floor as soon as he's through in there."

Then Terence drifted off again.

CHAPTER FOURTEEN

In the Grizzly Bar Myra kept watching for Iris and Jack. They'd be coming in after the opera, Iris had said, with some friends she wanted Myra to meet. But they didn't come, though Myra played Bach and New Orleans and Chicago until most of the people who had come in after the theatre and after the opera had left. Myra was sorry not to see Iris and the others. She was feeling a little forlorn again, in need of cheering. Something had happened somewhere, she gathered from snatches of conversation she overheard. A hold-up, was it, a shooting of some kind, near the Opera House? She didn't catch the details.

Max stopped in at closing time and she poured him a nightcap in her dressing room. "Here's to you, Myra," he said. "And here's to the samble. How are rehearsals going?"

Myra said she wasn't sure. "Iris isn't nearly up to Jack as a dancer," she said. "But they do something that audiences always love in a team—they give the impression of being crazy about each other. Maybe that and their good looks will put them over. *Are* they crazy about each other, do you know? I know he is about her, because he told me so, and she gives the impression she reciprocates. Does she, do you happen to know?"

Max had no idea. He seemed a little out of sorts tonight too. "I'm not their agent," he said, crossly. "Just yours. And as yours I don't like it when I ask you how the samble's going for you to tell me about them instead of about yourself. What's the matter, Myra? As an artist you should evaluate yourself more highly. The critics evaluate you, don't forget."

Myra shrugged and said nothing, and Max didn't stay long. "Remember, you're valuable to *me*," he said, swallowing his brandy. "Please relax. Here—here's a couple of newspapers to read yourself to sleep with. One from last night already and an early one of this morning yet. . . ."

At two o'clock Miss Quinn hadn't gone to bed. She sat at her desk, writing, crossing out, rewriting. What an evening! She hoped Terence wouldn't suffer too much. The wound was more painful than serious, the doctor had said when he'd finally come out from delivering that baby. Lucky the gun hadn't been aimed lower. What an awful thing! But then . . . more important things than the mere shooting of Terence had happened this evening. Miss Quinn felt very differently indeed about her nephew since reading that newspaper article. A Parisian love-nest! So she'd misjudged him! And the beautiful sound of those flutes . . . Miss Quinn thought condescendingly of her sister May and of Mount St. Margaret's. Mount St. Margaret's indeed! She wrote and scratched, wrote and scratched. The fewer words the better, and yet she had to be clear and expressive. . . .

CHAPTER FIFTEEN

"But you can't *do* this to me," Mr. Krebs almost wept into the mouthpiece.

"Indeed?" The Inspector inquired. "Can't I really? And anyway don't be so stuck on yourself. Nobody's doing anything *to you*. It's a question of doing something *for* somebody else—in this case for one of the newspaper boys. We owe them a little consideration— after all, they do favors for us sometimes."

"But the false pretenses . . ."

"What false pretenses? McSweeny said he was attached to headquarters. He is. He even gave his right name—a pretty well known name, too, to anybody that knows anything about police reporting. That was mighty fair of him. And if our absent-minded professor had exercised his citizen's prerogative and asked to see the man's badge, he'd have found out the truth for himself. Sorry—in my estimation it's all been perfectly open and above-board."

It was impressive to watch Mr. Krebs—as Terence watched him from his bed in the hospital Friday morning—gradually adjust himself to what was clearly a not exactly satisfactory reaction at the other end of the line.

In his farewells he achieved positive cordiality, and when he had hung up he turned to Terence with a sigh. "It takes a lot of effort sometimes to understand the other person's point of view. I must say I sympathize with the Inspector. As he says, a public official nowadays is helpless, helpless, without the good will of the press. . . ."

It was at precisely that point, with a few harsh words, that Terence took over his own case.

Not that Mr. Krebs lost any of his dignity or compassion in dismissal. "Don't think I hold you responsible for this outburst, dear boy. You're not yourself. How could you be? Pain, nerves . . . When you feel better, just telephone me. Summon me at any hour. . . ."

Shortly thereafter Mr. Harwood arrived, claiming— not too convincingly—to be apologetic about the errand that brought him. "But it's a tribute to your intelligence, Kelly, that I don't feel more apologetic than I do. I have confidence in your realizing that by now the thing's inevitable. Here—I've got it all typed out for you on Classics Department stationery. Shall we get it over with? All you have to do is sign."

Terence signed, and Mr. Harwood immediately took the document from him. "Many thanks," he said. "Very co-operative of you. We want to have it available for instant use, but actually we're not going to put it through until you're indicted. So you'll be on the payroll a few more days. We've been influenced in this decision by the fact that some of the women students got wind that your resignation was going to be asked for, and drew up a petition. Quite a few signatures, actually. It begs the university not to 'disgrace itself' by firing a man before he's been legally connected with the affair he's being fired for. Most unrealistic, of course: it ignores the whole unfavorable publicity side of things—the way you've gone and got Mr. Ramsay into the papers as well as yourself. But we don't want any bad blood on the campus, so we'll just put the resignation on file. You probably noticed that it's undated. I'll fill the date in myself when the time comes. I'll let you know, of course. . . ."

And Mr. Harwood had barely left and Terence had barely had time to tell the nurse rather wearily that he wanted no more visitors, when the telephone rang. The nurse took the message. "The Inspector," she reported, when she'd hung up. "He says that considering your condition he'll allow you a few more days to get that alibi. Up to a week, even. He wants to be fair."

"Very good of him. By the way, how long am I going to be kept in the hospital?"

"Well—I could be fired for telling you, you know, but the doctor says two weeks anyway. . . ."

PART THREE

CHAPTER ONE

The McSweeny piece, featured in one of the newspapers which Max had given Myra to read herself to sleep with, had not had that desired effect. She had wept through the rest of the darkness and well into the daylight in her room at the Park-Yorkshire. Most of her tears had been for herself, naturally. Tears of humiliation and resentment at the discovery that there had been someone with whom Terence had been able to let himself go, whereas with her he turned out to have been considerably more reserved than she had ever thought. That hurt her. And yet some of her tears were for Terence, too: tears for him because of the illumination which the article, despite its cheap intent, cast on his behavior; and tears for what his feelings must be in reading it.

The article made several things clear, if what it said was true. Above all, the fact that she had met Terence at a worse time in his life than she—or even he—had realized. She had tried to help him in Paris with his feelings of loneliness and guilt after his mother's death, but she hadn't understood the dense background of those feelings—she herself was one of a casually brought-up brood of children who had scattered early to shift for themselves and had never been in need of complicated understanding of their parents. All she had known up to today was that after what had seemed like a promising start between them, Terence had retreated into a baffling and wounding reserve. She was still wounded—more so than ever, at the moment—but not so baffled as she had been: how could the poor fellow have been expected to behave very differently? "Hands off the girls. . . ." Myra shook her head. What a precept! The death of such a mother, under such circumstances. . . . And in Terence's mind, of course, as is so often the case, various other reasons had conveniently come forward to screen the real ones.

And along with her resentment and humiliation at the news, and her tears for herself and Terence, Myra felt something that she hadn't felt for some time: hope. After all, it was no longer possible to think of Terence as always having been incapable of a closer relationship than theirs had ever been. And since he'd been capable of *one*, perhaps now if she acted wisely there was a chance that . . .

She telephoned Miss Quinn and suggested lunch again.

The two ladies embraced as usual when they met, but to her surprise Myra immediately sensed a coolness. Such a thing was so unexpected that she at first refused to recognize it; but after she had asked about Terence's wound and well-being and proceeded to other matters its existence was forced upon her. "This business about Terence and the affair in France," she said, as evenly as she could. "I didn't know about it, did you?"

"No."

"Is it true, do you suppose? The article's libelous, I should think, if . . ."

"It is true. Terence told me so at the hospital this morning. Except that the girl wasn't from the demi-monde at all. She was a perfectly nice little person from a . . ."

Myra winced—for some illogical reason she minded hearing that the girl had been nice—and then she noticed that Miss Quinn had broken off her sentence in the middle and was looking prim. "You were saying she was a perfectly nice little person, Aunt Kitty, from a . . ."

"Frankly, Myra . . ."

"Yes, Aunt Kitty?"

"Well . . . I don't want to be unkind, but I'm not sure I have the right to discuss Terence's affairs with you like this, that's all."

"Oh, I'm sorry. I thought that you and I . . ."

"You and I did think alike about Terence, and I did have all the sympathy in the world for you. But I was laboring under a delusion, just as you were. I was sorry for you being fond of somebody that seemed to be a . . . a priest, so to speak. When I was young the most tragic thing that could happen to a girl was to fall in love with a boy with a vocation. I thought that was happening to you, in a sense. I was sorry for you as I could be. But now . . ."

"Yes?"

"Well, the picture's changed, don't you see? Terence isn't the sort of person we supposed, at all. You don't imagine that girl in Paris has been the only one all this time, do you? Why, just last night when he was shot he was talking to a beauty at the Opera. A stunning girl. He'd never breathed a word of her existence to me. Only this morning did he barely mention her. So you see, my dear, in my opinion Terence has expressed a *preference*, and I don't feel privileged to interfere in any way. You do see what I'm driving at, don't you?"

Myra said she did.

"In a sense," said Miss Quinn, "it all boils down to the old question of knowing or not knowing how to get your man. And then of course there's the further question of knowing how to hold him, and, if you've let him go, knowing how to get him back. . . ."

Naturally Myra thought that Miss Quinn was still speaking, and quite outrageously, exclusively of her and Terence.

The rest of the lunch was rather strained. Momentarily forgetting Miss Quinn's ban on questions touching on her nephew, Myra asked about Jack Sanmartin, whose picture had been in the morning paper along with pictures of some of the others involved in the shooting. She told Miss Quinn about Jack being part of her act, and inquired as to the connection between Terence and the Sanmartins. Miss Quinn said there weren't any, except that the boy was in one of Terence's classes. "Terence just happened to introduce him to a girl, and he's fallen for her, and his father objects. Something like that. Actually," she said, possibly as a reproach to Myra for having asked her question, "the girl the boy's fallen for is *Terence's* girl. The beautiful one I mentioned. Her name's Iris."

Myra dropped her cigarette and disguised her agitation as best she could in a violent brushing of sparks and ashes. She could scarcely wait for lunch to be over, and the ladies exchanged mere handshakes and coolish glances as they parted.

Hurrying to her rehearsal, Myra felt herself on a kind of war-path. A Parisian love-nest in the past was one thing. But Iris as a rival right now . . .

CHAPTER TWO

Lulled by sedatives, Iris slept until nearly noon.

Out of solidarity the others had spent the night in her suite, one on the second twin bed and the other on the living-room sofa; and waking before her they made for the newspapers. There were no pictures of Iris: all the newspapers seemed luckily unaware of her connection with the affair. But there were excellent pictures of Terence on a stretcher, and of Mr. Sanmartin, dapper and collected-looking, being escorted to jail after refusing to state why he did the shooting; and there were especially excellent pictures of Jack. The boy looked worried—as well he might; but as Liz pointed out he also looked like an up-to-date and irresistible Valentino.

To the accompaniment of Iris's regular breathing they read and re-read the various accounts. The torn remains of the tiger-stripe dress and of their own gowns, lying as they'd been left the night before in piles on the floor, testified to the speed and violence of the departure from the opera bar which had prevented them from enjoying any leisurely view of the melee. "Several people seem to have been injured," Cynthia said. "This latest edition reports the mother and baby doing nicely. I bumped against at least a thousand people on my way out—I guess we all did. I'm sure that poor mother was one of them—it almost makes me feel responsible for what happened to her."

"I'd hate to find myself in such a place in such a condition," Liz said fervently, "or anywhere else, for that matter," and they shook their heads in wonderment at the ways of life chosen by other members of their sex.

When Iris finally woke, the tenseness of her questions made it clear that the sedative had worn off completely, and they hastened to give her a supplementary small dose, as the doctor had prescribed. "Where is Penn? Has he telephoned? How near had he got to me when the shot went off? What was the expression on his face?" Those were but a few of her inquiries. Cynthia and Liz could only answer that their maids, who had been instructed by telephone to pack daytime costumes which would be delivered to the Park-Yorkshire by chauffeur, had also been told to warn the butlers to expect calls from Mr. Penn-Gillis, whose number they were to take and whom they were to ask to telephone Mrs. Penn-Gillis at the hotel.

But when the telephone did ring, with Cynthia crying "Indifference!" as Iris lunged for the receiver, it proved to be only Zug, to say that he'd lost no time firing the Aiken operative for becoming "incapacitated" while on duty and letting Penn slip north without warning. He'd just hired a New York operative to search for Penn, who had disappeared following the shooting.

And then Iris had her breakfast, and then it was time for her to leave for the theatre.

CHAPTER THREE

Jack was the center of attention at the rehearsal, naturally. Everyone had expected that he'd stay away. But everyone was mistaken. He appeared on time, looking pale—as pale as he could look—and he replied gravely to kind greetings from members of the company.

"Sorry to read the news, Mr. Sanmartin."

"Thank you for your sympathy."

"Swell of you to show up, Jack."

"The show must go on."

He was serious-faced, low-voiced.

Everyone liked him for bringing his mother to the rehearsal. What a kind thing to do for the poor woman, instead of leaving her, shocked and upset, at home alone! A little diversion for her, a little something to take her out of her sorrow and bewilderment. He introduced a few people to her, escorting them to the orchestra seat where she was installed.

"Mama, this is Miss Drysdale, the harpsichordist, you know."

Myra was a little surprised by the "poor woman's" beaming smile, by her florid handshake and greeting. "I'm thrilled to meet you wonderful people. This is all so fascinating to me. I love this atmosphere. I know my son is so happy here, and where he's happy I'm happy."

Myra reminded herself that she didn't know all the facts, but wasn't there—even though nobody else in the theatre seemed to think so—something a bit monstrous about Mrs. Sanmartin's behavior under the circumstances?

During the early part of the rehearsal Myra was almost alone in paying any attention to Iris, but *her* attention was considerable.

"Hello, Myra darling."

"Hello, Iris dear."

It sounded as usual. But there was something in Myra's glance that Iris might have noticed if she hadn't been so extraordinarily absorbed in her own affairs. It was apparent to Myra, if to no one else, that today Iris was even more absorbed in her own affairs than usual.

This afternoon there was a particularly penetrating odor of narcissism about her—she seemed unable even to hear what people said until a half-minute or so after they had finished saying it. Something was going on inside Iris—no doubt about that.

And Myra, with her new knowledge, saw that whatever was going on had nothing to do with Jack. Iris paid no more attention to anything Jack said than she did to the remarks of others, and her gaze wandered away from Jack as it did from everybody else, and above all she wasn't dancing well. There was something wrong with Iris's samba today. Her feet and her body moved fairly well, but something important was missing. Jack, despite all that he'd gone through, was as absorbed in the dance and in Iris as ever, smiling at her and guiding her around the stage to Myra's tinkling rhythm; but today Iris no longer gave even the illusion of response—and self-absorption isn't attractive in a member of a dance team. Myra felt that she had her answer to the question she had asked Max, as to whether Iris returned Jack's interest. Obviously she didn't. Obviously, Myra saw, it wasn't Jack, but Terence, that Iris was infatuated with as she rolled and swayed in Jack's arms.

Myra's eyes narrowed as she fingered and pedaled her harpsichord, and for a moment she too was so absorbed in her own affairs that she didn't hear the dance director tell her to stop playing. When she finally obeyed him he addressed Iris. "Do you intend to stink opening night, too?" he inquired.

Iris burst into tears and ran off the stage, a handkerchief held to her face.

"Break for five minutes," the director said. "If she's not back by then we'll go on to something else."

"I don't see what there was for him to object to," said Mrs. Sanmartin to Jack and Myra as they sat beside her during the break. "I thought it was absolutely marvelous. I never saw anything so beautiful as everything everybody's doing. I've never enjoyed myself so much in my entire life. . . ."

CHAPTER FOUR

The first baby ever born in the Opera House received a more rousing welcome into the world, during his first few days, than most babies born in more usual places.

The Opera House press-agent was on the scene, or almost on the scene, the minute he heard what was happening: it isn't every day that a bit of unpleasant publicity like a shooting is immediately followed by an opportunity to neutralize it or even turn it to advantage. The press-agent looked piqued when the attendant refused him admittance to the Powder Room. "I suppose you're right," he reluctantly agreed. "I suppose I wouldn't be any more welcome in there now than at any other time. But I certainly hate to miss the best story of the season on account of a mere tabu." He proposed that he telephone his secretary and have her substitute for him, but just then the doctor came out and assured him that he needn't bother, for the event gave every indication of fulfilling itself in routine, uninteresting manner. "Talk to the father over there instead," he urged. "You'd be doing a kindness."

The press-agent obeyed. "Don't worry about expense," he said, as soon as he'd introduced himself to

Joe. "We'll take care of all that. Doctor, ambulance, hospital—don't give them another thought."

At any other time Joe might have had something to say to a stranger who walked up and offered him charity, but at the present moment he just smiled feebly and put a hand that was limp and damp into the outstretched hand of the press-agent.

The press-agent shook it vigorously. It was impossible to tell, of course, whether this young man, at present so pathetic and grateful, might not in a few weeks bring suit for enormous damages, complaining of physical and mental anguish of innumerable kinds suffered as the result of the Opera's negligence in permitting one of its patrons to enter the place armed. Some such brief as that might well be filed: the press-agent had seen many no less preposterous, and for most of them settlements of one kind or another had been devised. The only thing to do was to hope for the best, keep everyone as happy as possible, and meanwhile take advantage of the opportunity for acquiring merit that the situation offered. "I'd better telephone the hospital about a room," he said, "unless the doctor's done it already. Will the East Fifties Hospital be satisfactory? Is there any particular exposure your wife prefers?"

He felt a little better about things an hour or so later, when everything was over and the baby was crying and Joe gave him a hand that was even damper and limper than it had been, and told him he'd never forget his kindness in standing by. "I'd have gone nuts without you," he said, his voice booming out in the vastness of the bar, now dim and deserted except for an attendant or two. "Absolutely nuts." That was something. It was an admission, before witnesses, that the Opera House had done what it could in the emergency. It offered no assurance against suit, of course, but it was something, a straw in the wind.

And then the Powder Room door opened and a procession came out: doctor, nurse holding baby, mother on stretcher, ambulance men. "I'll come along to the hospital, too," the press-agent said. "Just to be sure everything's all right."

Joe followed him like a big grateful dog.

The next afternoon, when Joe could see that Sadie and the baby were doing well and that there was nothing to worry about, he looked worried anyway and asked Sadie whether she thought it was really a good idea for them to accept what the Opera House offered.

Sadie said she thought it an excellent idea. They had been promised special rates at the hospital where she had worked, but in her opinion no rates at all were even better. "We'll save at least a couple of hundred dollars," she said. "That means almost a term's tuition at college. Why, he's nearly halfway through his freshman year already."

"You're probably right—the poor little bastard sure looks like he's been through a hazing."

"He does not. He looks sweet. *Sweet*."

"Well . . . *You* do, anyway."

About that time the nurse started bringing in large vases of flowers, chiefly roses, and with each bunch was the card of one or another of the singers whom they had heard the night before in *The Magic Flute*. And then she came in again and surprised them by saying "The manager of the Opera House is outside, and the press-agent, and a lot of singers and newsreelers. Of course they can't come in here, but the doctor says there's no reason for them not to take pictures of the baby through the glass wall of the nursery if you don't object.

"Well," Joe said, turning red, "I certainly do ob . . ."

"I don't," said Sadie, quickly. "And please don't you. Something tells me he's going to be a sophomore any minute. Don't keep him from being promoted."

So the nurse lifted the baby and took it out to the nursery, and Joe, breathing deeply and making Sadie laugh with his look of martyrdom, walked out into the hall and let the press-agent introduce him to the manager and the singers. At first it was no ordeal because everyone ignored him. The singers, busy arranging themselves at the nursery window, barely acknowledged his introduction: it was complicated to get them all fairly placed and yet leave a clear view of the baby in the bassinet, with room for the manager near the middle of the group. But then, when everything was ready, the press-agent placed Joe, sweating and gulping, on the other side of the mike from the manager, and one of the newsreel men whispered "You're on," and the manager, a dignified gentleman in striped trousers, smiled a camera-smile at Joe and said, in booming tones that were broadcast far and wide, "Well, Mr. Giuliano, how's the air up there?"

For weeks afterwards Joe woke up nights reliving his cowardice of that moment, his gulping, feeble "Very good, thank you, sir . . ." just as if he were back in the Pacific, answering some lousy officer.

"And I want to give my personal assurance," the manager was saying, when Joe came sufficiently out of his daze to hear again, "that if this first baby ever born in the Opera House shows signs of possessing musical talent, I personally will see that he receives the finest musical education that money can buy. That is my personal guarantee, before witnesses. And whether he does or not, I wish to offer him, on behalf of these fine artists here with me, this birthday present, a token of the es-

teem in which his brief existence is already held by those
of us at the Opera House." And he handed Joe an envelope he had been holding, and Joe gulped again and
said "Thank you, sir, very, very much," and the singers,
all smiling intently into the camera, burst out into
"Where Did You Come From, Baby Dear?" And then
somebody waved an arm and it was over and once again
nobody paid the slightest attention to Joe and all went
their own ways.

"Just one shot through the door, of the mother in
bed with the baby, and all those roses around?" the
press-agent begged a doctor who had stopped to watch.
"Just one, please?" The doctor looked at Joe, and Joe,
feeling the envelope between his fingers, nodded his
head, and the doctor nodded his. . . .

After everyone had gone Joe opened the envelope and
showed the contents to Sadie. She counted on her fingers. "Good Lord—he's in his senior year, as far as tuition is concerned," she told Joe. "Almost graduated already. I can even scare up a few kindly feelings toward
that professor, at this rate. After all, if he hadn't been
shot . . ."

CHAPTER FIVE

Terence had plenty of time and incentive, during
his first day or two in the hospital, to reflect again and
yet again on the consequences of the new program, as
he saw them. His considerable physical wincings whenever the doctor probed and dressed his wound were so
very much less painful than his spiritual wincings when-

ever he thought of the McSweeny piece, which was most of the time, that he forced himself to read the outrage over and over again, seeking in its very horridness some clue to what had gone so wrong. A program of detachment, primarily designed to separate oneself from others, and resulting instead in the blazoning of one's most private past in the public prints . . . In comparison with that, the as yet not wholly explained but obviously heart-felt vituperation of Iris, the murderous rage of Mr. Sanmartin, the premature birth of a baby to a young couple, his probable loss of his job, and the receipt of one week of grace in which to extract from a lunatic the alibi which alone would keep him from being indicted for murder, whereas for that week and longer he was to be confined to a bed in a hospital at the other end of the city from the hospital containing the lunatic in question—all those seemed comparatively minor miscarriages of his program. Not that they *were* minor. Terence recognized that they were scarcely that, especially in the aggregate. He found it difficult to take them all in, and he suspected that that might be because they were, in fact, so very major: but in any case the wounds they had inflicted seemed to be of the numbing variety, whereas the McSweeny piece . . . There was nothing numbing about what *that* did to him.

Sometimes, when he was able to keep from reading or thinking about it for a few consecutive minutes, he devoted himself as he lay in bed to a slightly different occupation, also on the cheerless side, but in which, just as in reading the McSweeny piece, he sensed that he might find a clue to the disaster: he considered, in turn, and in so far as he was able, each of the persons or groups with whom he had, out of careful choice, spent his birthday, the day of the inauguration of the program.

The associations, that is, which he had considered so
choice because of their non-entangling character, and
concerning which he had congratulated himself on his
way home from Ramsay's that night. His colleagues, first
of all, who had in their professional capacity merely rendered a favorable verdict on his thesis—and returned it
to him, so that he had it with him that day, to leave at
Cynthia's. His students: and in amongst them Jack Sanmartin, whose enthusiasm had been aroused by words
in praise of Vergil. The milliner. The Three—or at least
two of them, so far: Cynthia who had been his unwit-
ting betrayer, and now Iris. And finally Ramsay, the
paragon of aloofness and non-entanglement. A sorry
list—painful to contemplate.

Whereas the other list, the shorter list—that of the
individuals with whom he had deliberately *not* spent
his birthday . . . What of them?

There was no doubt that had he spent his birthday
evening with his aunt, as she had wanted him to, he
would not now be in all his difficulties. Unlike poor
Ramsay, Miss Quinn had not gone mad, and though
the first splurge of newspaper publicity could probably
not have been avoided, she would at least have furnished him an alibi, the McSweeny piece would never
have been written, and his resignation would not now
be on file at the university. Aunt Kitty's frequent "If
only's" Terence found in retrospect a good deal less irritating than poignant. What was strange was not that
she should have said "If only . . ." so often, but that
she now seemed to have stopped saying it at all. Not
once, for example—though she certainly must know how
he felt—had she commiserated with him on the Mc-
Sweeny piece. She spoke soothingly of his wound on
each of her daily visits to the hospital. But to his chief
indignity she never referred. "If only you'd spent your

birthday with me, Terence; you wouldn't have this nasty old newspaper article to fret about." What would have come more naturally from her lips than that? But it didn't come. Just another bafflement among the debris resulting from the total miscarriage, as Terence now recognized it to be, of the program.

And then there was Myra.

Had he spent his birthday evening with her the results would doubtless have been the same as had he spent it with his aunt; and furthermore, if the program was the general disaster it seemed to be, perhaps the Myra part of it was just as mistaken as the rest. So . . . There was something to think about there.

But there was the indictment to think about first.

When he could, he telephoned Ramsay.

"Terence! where *have* you been? They tell me you were shot or something. Is it true?"

"Yes, I was shot. Not seriously, but . . ."

"My, my! I must say I've been feeling neglected. Not that I've had anything to report. I've got nowhere. Haven't advanced a step since our interesting talk the other day. By the way, how's your friend McSweeny? A courteous fellow. The older I get the more I like that quiet, attentive kind of student. . . ."

"Ramsay . . ."

"I'm almost beginning to wish I'd never taken up this *Muscipula Diaboli* thing. Some mysteries have no solution, you know, and humiliating though it is to say so I'm beginning to fear . . ."

"Ramsay, listen: do you think the reason for the absence of the mousetrap in the last picture might be this? That by the time of the scene it portrays—Joseph's old age—Christ had already been crucified? In other words, the devil had already been caught and there was no reason for a trap any more?" Terence had a momentary feeling of mirth at the thought of two academics sitting at opposite ends of a telephone line talking about symbolic mousetraps.

Sounds of scorn came over the wire. "Terence! Are you illiterate? In the first place don't you see that had the painter wished to convey that idea he would have shown a *sprung* mousetrap instead of *no* mousetrap? There's nothing pictorial about *no* mousetrap, whereas a *sprung* one, with probably a dead little mouse in it, painted so as to bring to mind a tiny trapped little devil, with long ears and a tail . . . Can you *see* it? Isn't it *horrible?* Surely that's how that idea would have been portrayed, Terence. And in the second place you seem to forget that all the traditions indicate that Joseph was dead by the time of the Crucifixion. The Gospels tell us that Mary was present at the foot of the Cross, but there's never a mention of Joseph. So it's assumed that he'd passed away before. No, the panel showing the death of Joseph can't very well be interpreted as representing an episode taking place after the death of Christ, since Joseph's death came first. Absolutely impossible, Terence. It won't wash. Not a chance. When are you coming to see me?"

"As soon as I can. I think they'll let me out in a week or so."

"Let you *out?* Out of what? Where are you?"

"In a hospital."

"But I thought it was *I* who was in a hospital, Terence! What *is* this? What's the matter, Terence, with me and you . . . ? Where are we? Who's responsible for our being here? I know, I think. I know, and I hate her. I hate all those masterful mothers. . . ."

Ramsay started whimpering, and Terence spent a little time doing his best to reassure him about their situations before hanging up.

He sat there pondering for a moment. Ramsay's last words had suddenly, he suspected, given him a new and true light on the wretched new program. "Hands off!" Didn't those words that had turned out so badly owe their origin, in some obscure psychic way, to those other, similar words, so often uttered by his mother, and also unfavorable in their result: "Hands off the girls"? As soon as this idea came to him there seemed little doubt that it was correct; and Terence reflected that it was high time to forget, or rather to abjure, both his mother's words and their equally unfortunate offspring.

He was more than a little depressed by the badness of his mousetrap guess. Especially since he'd begun to suspect that there might be a connection of some kind between a solution of that mystery and a solution of his own predicament—which he was enjoying less and less every hour. He thought a bit, then telephoned the university library and spoke at length with people in the reference room and at the loan desk.

CHAPTER SIX

Gus was in Milwaukee when he saw the notice.

Taking his ease as he always did on a Saturday afternoon, sitting in one of the row of rocking chairs inside the big plate-glass window of the Pfister House Hotel, his feet up on the window-sill so that the soles of his shoes were available for inspection by all the passers-by on Water Street. Smoking his pipe and reading the *Pickle Gazette*. And there was the notice, just as for seven years he'd thought with varying degrees of faith that some day it might be. Except that he'd never expected it to be right on the front page, headed "Special: received too late for classification."

"Gus: please come home. All is forgiven and all shall be as you so desire."

It was the second part of the second sentence that had caused Miss Quinn her great travail: not so much its wording—though she had struggled hard to give it just the right emotional tone—as its very inclusion. It was the hauling down of her flag, and even under the impact of her sister's letter and of all of Mozart's flutes and the news of Terence's old liaison Miss Quinn didn't find that an easy thing to do. Was any man, even Gus, worth such surrender as that? She wrote, crossed out, and rewrote for hours before she was finally able to assure herself that he was. Then she'd gone out and dropped the envelope into the corner mailbox, and hadn't fallen asleep till dawn.

". . . all shall be as you so desire. . . ." Gus felt a chill go up and down his spine as he read the words: a chill that accompanied the brain-picture he immediately conceived, of Kitty, seven years older than she'd been in Yonkers, actually sitting down and writing them.

The other men sitting in the row of rocking chairs, smoking their pipes or cigarettes or cigars, making use from time to time of the Pfister House spittoons and reading their equivalents of the *Pickle Gazette*—the *Shoeman's Weekly* or the *Rubber Goods Review*—suddenly seemed miles away to Gus. Poor fellows! No little lady in New York had sat down and written *them* a message saying "All shall be as you so desire." Drab, dreary derelicts! Money in the bank, perhaps, just as he had, but nothing to do, on Saturday afternoons and Sundays, except sit as they were sitting, year in and year out. Gus had sat with them for seven years, but it had just taken him less than seven seconds to dissociate himself from them. He continued to sit and smoke his pipe very quietly, pretending to read the rest of the *Pickle Gazette* as usual but actually reading and re-reading only the little notice, and betraying to none of the others in the slightest degree the fact that he was no longer really there at all.

Well! What was to be done? What should be the first step? A little remorse, that he was not returning to Kitty quite as clean as he had left her? Yes, a *little* remorse over that, perhaps, but not more than a little. For if Kitty, instead of waiting seven years to call him back, had said to him "All shall be as you so desire" before he'd even left, he wouldn't have walked out of the Yonkers apartment into the arms of the kind of girls he'd never associated with before in his life. Not that before meeting Kitty on the pier in Atlantic City he'd associated with angels: as he'd told her at the time, she was something different for him, so different that he'd insisted on the ceremony. But the kind of girls he'd gone to from the Yonkers apartment . . . ! Gus shuddered at the memory. It was a nasty thing for Kitty's baptism mania to be responsible for, that period of . . . of depravity. That was the only word for it. And it only went to confirm what Gus had always thought of religion in general ever since he'd first read Robert Ingersoll when he was sixteen years old, a hose-boy in the stockyards in Chicago. Religion and evil went hand in hand. They always did—they always would. Fortunately Gus hadn't kept going with those girls very long. So that for two reasons—first because it was Kitty's religion that was really responsible, and second because of the brevity of the debauch—he needn't feel too large-scale a remorse. Since pulling himself out of that mess he'd reverted to the sort of thing he'd gone in for before meet-

ing Kitty: perfectly decent, clean interludes—chiefly
follow-ups of contacts made in the normal course of the
pickle-business—interludes that nobody in his right
mind could be ashamed of, but which nevertheless
lacked some of the appeal they had once had, for a man
who had since known what it was to live in a household
of his own.

So . . . What next, after the certain amount of remorse—which was pretty much over already, now that
he'd thought about it. A telegram to Kitty? A telephone
call? Once again a chill went up and down his spine, at
the thought that in five minutes or even less, if he
wanted to, he could be listening to Kitty's voice in one
of the Pfister House telephone booths not five yards
away. A Circle telephone number was the notice's signature. All he had to do was to call it, and . . .

But somehow Gus did not spring out of his chair and
dial Long Distance. Something restrained him. What
was it? Lethargy? Cowardice? A desire to prolong this
moment, which had a particularly delicious quality
about it—a quality that made him feel free, lighter than
air, floating between two worlds, released from one of
them and not yet attached to the other? Immensely superior to the poor derelicts in the other rocking chairs,
and yet so far not committed to anything. . . .

CHAPTER SEVEN

The bartender in the Hibernia Bar and Grille
wasn't surprised to see that the red-headed balloon-seller
was back in his groove. The only wonder was that he'd

stayed out of it as long as he had. Ten days or so, wasn't it? Quite a stretch, for a fellow like the redhead.

A series of drinks at the bar, a tendency to be loud-voiced with the other drinkers, and then a fairly quick exit with a goal apparently in mind: that was the groove the redhead had followed for months. And then it had suddenly changed to no drinks, a morose and solitary meal in one of the booths, and an aimless-seeming departure, with backward, longing glances in the direction of the bar. Tonight not only was he drinking again, but he'd gone at his glass so quickly that he hadn't even taken off the gloves he'd been wearing when he came in with his balloons. And not only had he grasped his first glass with gloves on, but now his fingers were still gloved as they clasped his third or fourth.

"Special interest in the case," he was saying rather jerkily to his neighbor. "Book-binder myself."

The neighbor, who had had as many as Red, if not more, half-closed his eyes and nodded vaguely.

"Balloons just sideline, help out bad times."

Nobody could have had any idea of the amount of pleasure the redhead was getting out of saying just those things about himself. Before Helene's death Red had so constantly called himself a book-binder that almost without realizing it he'd come to think of himself as one. Since her death he'd found reversion to the role of mere balloon-seller one of the most trying of the changes he'd had to put up with. Tonight his endurance had finally come to an end. "Sure," he said. "Binder myself. Give you my card, had one with me. At first thought other binder guilty man. You know—Giuliano. Friends, them two. Get what I mean?"

"Giuliano?" said the neighbor, thickly. "Don't remember reading *that* name in the papers."

"Sure. Kid born in Opera House. Picture in hospital."

"Oh, that fella. But don't remember reading he had any connection with the milliner."

"Sure he had. Police know all about it. Protecting him, don't know why. Dirty work someplace. Makes no difference. Changed my mind anyway. Binder didn't do it. Prof did it. You know—prof?"

"Sure—I seen about *him* in the papers."

"That afternoon, somebody come in—wouldn't wait. Said be back that night. Whoever *that* was, last person see her alive."

"Didn't read *that* in the papers."

"I'm telling you. Look—see this? Says 'Professor Kelly admitted having visited the shop during the day.' Just putting two and two together. Prof come in, wouldn't wait, told her he'd be back that night. See point?"

"Howja know? Didn't read nothing in papers about nobody coming in that afternoon and saying he'd be back."

"God damn it! Wasn't *in* the papers. I'm telling you. Is only things that's in the papers true? Can't you take word of gentleman?"

"Where ya get ya infamation?"

"Aw, go ———— yaself. . . ."

Yes, the redhead was back in the groove. . . .

CHAPTER EIGHT

"A mouse's liver grows and wanes with the moon," Ramsay announced by telephone one morning. "Did you know that, Terence? Mouse droppings are an aphrodisiac. Mice aren't born—they appear by spontaneous generation out of excrement or a whirlwind. White mice are the incarnation of the souls of unborn children. Last night I read the article on mice in the *Handwörterbuch des deutschen Aberglaubens*, and it's given me the creeps. I had no idea of the erotic and diabolical meaning mice had in popular magic and folklore. A mouse is the womb, the unchaste female, the prostitute. For aid in anything concerning mice, Christians pray to St. Gertrude, a Belgian virgin descended from Apollo. I've been praying to her all night. I can't stand thinking about mice. Never could. No wonder I've failed with this *Muscipula Diaboli* thing: too upset by the subject-matter to do my best work. I *have* failed, Terence. I hereby give up. Formally. I never thought I'd be willing to leave a mystery unsolved, but I was wrong. I feel better just telling you my decision. After all, there's nothing that compels me or anybody else to solve the damnable thing. The subject is closed. *Closed*, do you understand?"

Terence's heart sank.

As soon as he was permitted to visit Professor Kelly the press-agent of the Opera House did so, to repeat in person what he had already said in a letter: that all expenses were being met and that he stood ready to perform any other desired services. His conception of the academic life was confirmed by the appearance of the professor's hospital room: the floor, the bed-table and the bed itself were littered with books, and the professor was examining, with a rather grim air, a forbidding volume of impressive size and thickness. He was also repeating in a mumble, as the press-agent entered, something that sounded like "St. Gertrude have mercy on us. St. Gertrude pray for us." He showed little interest in what the press-agent had to tell him about Mr. Sanmartin, whose family had refused to visit him in jail and who would soon be moving from one of the city lock-ups to the big house up the river. "The ironic thing is," the press-agent said, "he owns the theatre his son's show is opening in tonight—the show he couldn't stand the idea of. Owns lots of other places, too. Park-York-shire Hotel . . ."

The professor just nodded. Then he came out of his books long enough to inquire about other people. "What about *young* Sanmartin?" he asked.

The press-agent knew nothing but offered to investigate.

"And then that young couple—what's their name? The ones whose baby was born in the Opera House."

If the nurse hadn't stepped into the room just then the professor might well have been misled: for it was against the press-agent's principles to allow possible plaintiffs to get acquainted with one another—joint and group actions being the disagreeable things they are. "Some of the other girls and I saw that darling news-reel about the Giulianos last night," the nurse said, as the press-agent opened his mouth and shut it again. "We were so excited. Everybody downstairs just loves Mrs. Giuliano and the baby."

"I'd keep away from the Giulianos if I were you," the press-agent warned the professor. "I've been particularly careful not to tell them you were here in the hospital. I've been visiting them from time to time, and I've gath-ered from remarks I've overheard that they resent you rather strongly."

"I should think they would," said the professor. "Won't you ask the people downstairs," he said to the nurse, "to tell Mr. Giuliano that I'd appreciate it if he'd come up?"

Then he was back in his book again.

There was a certain awkwardness in the meeting of the two young men that night—an awkwardness on both sides. Terence was without training in the etiquette of apologizing to a father for having caused his baby to be born before its time, and Joe had been placed in a state of confusion by Sadie's last-minute coaching. "Don't let the professor get away with anything," she said severely. "Pin him down as to exactly why he said that about you and the milliner. Let him know what we think of him for saying such a thing. But remember—the first baby ever born in the Opera House is practically through college already due entirely to the professor's being shot. And remember the watchword: Be Polite."

As a result of those instructions and of his surprise at discovering the professor to be so much younger-looking than he had been led to expect by his title and the newspaper photographs, Joe found himself, during the silence that followed the first hesitant exchange of greetings, almost on the point of asking "What outfit were you with?" That was always the easiest question.

But the professor got there first. "What outfit were you with, Giuliano?" he asked, out of the silence.

They exchanged information on that subject for a little longer than they might have if either of them had been perfectly easy about what would come next.

Then Terence made the plunge. "I wanted to see you, Giuliano, to tell you that I feel a definite responsibility . . ."

"Good heavens, sir, it wasn't you that fired the shot and caused the crowd to stampede. . . ."

"No, but if I hadn't done certain things that you don't know about, that led up to it . . ."

They went thoroughly into the consequences that the shooting had had for the Giulianos. "Well, then," Terence said, "as long as everybody's health is all right and if you'll let me if only for the sake of my own conscience add a little something to the college fund . . ."

They were rapidly getting friendly—too friendly, Joe told himself, considering who this was. "Those things you say you did that led up to the shooting, sir," he said, struggling to observe all Sadie's instructions at once. "Those things you say I don't know about. Would any of them possibly be connected with . . ." But something happened when he got that far, and he began almost to shout. ". . . with that God damned lousy lie you told the Inspector?" he burst out, his face red and his voice angry as he thought of Sadie and himself and the baby and of how this heel had smeared them all.

Quite a little conversation took place—with Joe alternating between politeness and the extreme opposite and with Terence wondering at moments whether his visitor was crazy—before Terence fully realized that he was more closely connected with this young man than merely by ties of shooting and childbirth, and before Joe realized that the professor had had no idea of who he was and had never heard his name in connection with the case.

"So you're the binder!" Terence said, rubbing his forehead as though to rub away confusion. "But . . ." Some of the confusion seemed to remain, despite the rubbing. "Obviously I never told the Inspector you were intimate with the milliner," he said. "I never told him anybody was, because I didn't *know* that anybody was. And yet now that I think of it I do seem to remember getting the impression that *somebody* was intimate with her. Who could it have been, if not you? You were the only person we talked about, except when she urged me to come in again with my girl-friend. Still . . ."

There was something wrong someplace.

And then all at once it was Joe's turn to wonder

whether someone was crazy. "Listen," said the professor, suddenly, sitting up straight. "Listen, Giuliano: are you Irish?"

"Me *Irish?*"

"Yes—or *were* you Irish? And have you got red hair or *did* you have red hair? Oh, 'Me rid-hidded Oirish byfrind!' Hand me that phone, Giuliano!"

Over the wire Terence's voice conveyed his excitement more clearly than his meaning, and the Inspector replied benevolently. "You say you've just met the black-haired binder with the Italian name and you suddenly remember he's a red-headed Irishman after all? That's wonderful, Professor, wonderful. What can I do for you? Send you up with your friend in the Medical Center?" The Inspector hung up without any very formal farewells.

Joe went to headquarters at once. He gave the Inspector a clear account of what Terence remembered, and he added a few observations of his own. They flagrantly disobeyed Sadie's watchword and the advice of the lawyer from the Legal Aid Society: under ordinary circumstances he would have been locked up immediately for abusive language. But the Inspector sensed progress in the case at last and felt lenient. He thought it wiser, under the circumstances, not to try to explain that Mr. Giuliano had "misunderstood" him concerning the intimacy informant. He simply took the anonymous letter out of a file and showed it to Joe. "Probably written by a red-headed Irishman without fingerprints," he said. "If we find him, it looks like we're through. That is, of course, if the prof produces an alibi. . . ."

"Was I right about trouble being good for the professor?" the Inspector asked his men complacently when Joe had gone. "A night in jail and a newspaper story, and he remembered that the binder was expected that night. Now another newspaper story and a bullet in the shoulder and he remembers the color of the binder's hair. Time for more stimulation, wouldn't you say? Can't think of anything good off-hand: just let's remind him in print about inevitable indictment at the end of the week if his alibi's still missing. Get it into the morning papers, will you? And now go out and arrest every red-headed Irish book-binder you see that looks as though he writes anonymous letters with gloves on."

CHAPTER NINE

It all happened so fast and so bewilderingly that Myra wasn't quite sure *what* had happened. Had there been an opening Monday night? Apparently so: at least there were notices in the Tuesday morning papers. The dramatic critic of the *Times* was awfully kind:

"The high spot in the revue for this commentator was the playing of a glorified Brazilian samba on an outraged but wonderfully responsive harpsichord, by the invaluable Myra Drysdale. Hitherto praise of Miss Drysdale has been the prerogative, in the columns of this newspaper, of those concerned with the goings-on in night-clubs and concert halls: the present writer wishes to express his thanks to whoever is responsible for at last bringing Miss Drysdale under his jurisdiction. . . . Being so completely entranced by Miss Drysdale's performance, to the point of half-expecting the harpsichord itself to start dancing a samba, so marvellously intense and evocative were the changing rhythms and tempi that Miss Drysdale induced it to utter, we perhaps paid less attention than we ordinarily might have to the young couple calling themselves Iris and Jack who actually did the dancing. But since a telephone call from her agent has just informed us that in future performances Miss Drysdale and her harpsichord will appear alone, without benefit of human dancers, we shall merely say discreetly that although both Jack and Iris were very good-looking, only one of them struck us as being a dancer. . . ."

There was no doubt as to which member of the team the *Times* critic meant: most of the other papers mentioned Iris unkindly by name. And no wonder: what a performance she had given! During the final rehearsals she had been bad enough—the dance director had threatened to resign unless she improved, thus confirming the cast's suspicion that she was non-dismissable. But the dance director hadn't resigned, and it was just as well that he hadn't, for immediately after Iris's opening-night performance, which was a thousand times worse than any she had given before, a note had been delivered to her dressing room and she'd rushed out of the theatre without a word to anyone. She'd driven off in a limousine with a gentleman in it that was waiting outside the stage-door alley, the doorman said, and that was the last that was known of her.

And Jack Sanmartin, who with his mother and a gentleman not connected with the show had been standing near by and seen Iris rush silently away, had smiled and said "Well, Mama, I guess that means we can leave for the coast tomorrow." He introduced Myra to the gentleman, who asked her if she too wouldn't be interested in traveling west. "I can't offer you anything like the gorgeous contract I'm giving Jack, naturally. He's got real screen appeal. But we ought to be able to squeeze you into a one-spot novelty number someplace," he said, with the tact usual to such individuals. Myra told him to get in touch with Max.

"I'm so glad the Hollywood offer came through," she said to Mrs. Sanmartin as the others retired to confer in the privacy of one of the backstage telephone booths. "It will help take Jack's mind off Iris—I know how he feels about her."

"Felt, you mean."

"Oh?"

"Last week, perhaps, a little. But now . . . How could he? Such a disappointing artiste. Jack has his career to think of. Over the week-end we had long talks about what was the best thing to do. Jack feared that to make his debut with such a partner might be disastrous, but on the other hand she was giving him the chance to appear right away. He decided definitely to go ahead with it after we began to hear rumors about Hollywood's reaction to those pictures of Jack in the papers. Frankly, we hoped and prayed that some offer like this would turn up to let us leave for the coast at once. Because from out there we can testify in writing. You know what I'm referring to?"

"Yes. I'm so sorry."

"Oh, that's all right, my dear. When you're absent on legitimate business it's permissible to testify in writing. It's so much easier; you just have a lawyer take down your testimony and then forget about the whole thing. Forget it for ten or fifteen years, I imagine—less the time he'll get off for good behavior, of course. That's what the lawyers tell us the sentence is likely to be. I do so look forward to sunshine and Hollywood. . . ."

Then Max appeared and seized Myra's hands and kissed her on both cheeks. "The audience was besides itself," he said, reverently. "I was afraid for the building, their clap was so terrible. I almost imagined I heard the walls begin to shitter." He wouldn't even talk with the Hollywood gentleman. "He's a procurator," he said, scornfully, lowering his voice out of consideration for Mrs. Sanmartin. "A pimple for the movies. All right for a pretty boy dancer, but for an artist . . . Don't soil yourself, Myra." And after disappearing for a while he came back to say that the producer wanted her to stay in the show at the total salary that had been paid to all three members of the team. Then, after Myra took her curtain calls, they taxied to the Park-Yorkshire. Numerous people who had been at the theatre were in the Grizzly Bar, and there were calls for "Samba! Samba!" and an even more enthusiastic atmosphere than usual. And in the *Times* the next morning, in addition to the dramatic critic's notice, there was a paragraph about her in the night-club column:

"Such devotion to art as that shown by Miss Myra Drysdale—and whatever she plays on her harpsichord *is* art, whether it be Correlli or a Samba—is, alas, usually paid for by the artist in one form or another of sacrifice or suffering. So it has been since the world began. At the Grizzly Bar last night after her triumphant debut on the boards, we thought Miss Drysdale did not look as well as usual. Perhaps it was a mere temporary fatigue, due to the strain of the evening. Being devotees of Miss Drysdale's, we sincerely trust it was no more."

Myra blushed when she read that. For it hadn't been fatigue that had caused her to feel, at the Grizzly Bar, the way the night-club reporter said she had looked. It had been the thought of that "limousine with a gentleman in it" that Iris had rushed out to and been driven off in. Myra knew that Terence, in bed in the hospital, wasn't driving around in limousines. So it wasn't Terence that Iris had driven off with, and so it wasn't Terence, after all, that Iris had been mooning about all this time! And therefore it hadn't been necessary for Myra to keep changing the rhythms and tempi of the samba during the opening-night performance the way she had. Jack hadn't been thrown off in the slightest by her improvisations—there wasn't a rhythm or tempo in the world, probably, that Jack couldn't adapt himself to instinctively. But poor Iris. . . . All the time she played in the Grizzly Bar Myra kept thinking of Iris's false starts and stops, her uncertain recoveries, the look of bewilderment on her beautiful face as she wondered what in the world was happening to the music she was trying to dance to. And it hadn't been necessary to do it! It hadn't been necessary to break anything up—or at least have a little revenge—by making Iris ridiculous and getting her even worse notices than she deserved! Because there hadn't been anything to break up. Terence, whatever *his* feelings might be, hadn't been in the running with Iris. And she herself, therefore, had no rival. . . .

No rival! She was almost sorry to learn it. It had been so concrete, for a brief while, trying to get Terence back from somebody else. Whereas now everything was just depressing again. And things looked bad, too. For Terence, as well as she, was mentioned in the morning paper. Just a short statement: "It was announced at headquarters last night that Professor Terence Kelly, in the absence of an alibi, is definitely facing indictment within a few days in connection with the recent Fifty-Seventh

Street murder." And there was nothing, nothing, that she could do. . . .

CHAPTER TEN

Miss Quinn tried to do some shopping on her way to the hospital Tuesday morning.

But neither in Brentano's periodical department nor at the big news-stand in Times Square did she find what she wanted. The newsdealer suggested the Public Library, but even there she found no *Pickle Gazette*. She felt frustrated, for she was eager to see whether the notice had been printed. If it had arrived too late, and been held over to the next issue, she wanted to know it, so that she could stop fretting. She thought of visiting the office of a pickle company, even of *the* pickle company, but she couldn't quite bring herself to. She had met a good many of the pickle people, years ago. They had a way, she knew, of changing back and forth from one company to another, and whatever company she went to someone might recognize her. No! better not. Better wait as patiently as possible.

At the hospital she told Terence of an unexpected house-guest who was occupying one of her rooms.

"I feel sad about him," she said. "He's my own flesh and blood even if I do think so little of his parents. In his pyjamas this morning he looked and acted just like any other boy—it was almost like having you in the house again, Terence, snorting and splashing in the bathroom. Then he put on his black suit and that collar . . . Well, I wish I'd got hold of him about ten years ago."

Terence put aside the newspaper. His aunt, he was glad to see, gave no indication of having read it, and he didn't tell her of the reminder of his plight which it contained. "How does Vinny happen to be in New York, did you say, Auntie? I wasn't quite listening, I'm afraid. Isn't he a curate someplace by now?"

"He's about to be. At a new church just a block away from his family. He's here on a week's vacation with a couple of his pals from the seminary. He's never been in New York before, except passing through incommunicado on his way overseas a few years ago. That's typically Mahony: neither May nor her husband's ever been out of the state of Massachusetts, so far as I know. He brought me a typically Mahony message, too. His mother wants to be sure I realize she had no ulterior motive in writing that letter to Mount St. Margaret's. She wants me to know that if I prefer to leave my money to a Home instead of to my family, it's entirely up to me. She's not avaricious. It was just that she felt morally obligated to let them know they might be admitting a mortal sinner. It was her religious duty. I was so sorry for Vinny while he stood there telling me all that. He looked so embarrassed. I just patted his hand and told him not to worry about me. I think he must be nicer than the rest of them, to be so unprejudiced against his immoral old aunt. He had a hotel room all reserved, but he seemed awfully pleased when I asked him to stay."

Terence asked with more politeness than enthusiasm whether he'd be seeing his cousin.

"He's crazy to meet you. He says he's afraid, though —you're such a scholar. He claims they'd have flunked him out of the seminary the very first term if they hadn't needed him on the football team. This morning he's off with his friends on one of those sight-seeing trips around the city. He said he'd try to drop in on you later in the day.

"Do be nice to Vinny, Terence," Miss Quinn urged when she rose to go. "I mean, we've had so much family disharmony it would be lovely if you two could get along. Be glad your one and only cousin seems to be a *nice* boy. Don't be too hard on him for not being bright."

Terence assured her he was in no mood, these days, to feel superior to a cousin or anyone else on that account.

Jack Sanmartin surprised him with a visit at noon. He seemed breathless, and declined Terence's offer of a lunch tray. "I know I should have come in long ago," he said, "but I've been so busy. I assure you I would have come in today even if I hadn't had a call from the Opera House saying you'd been asking for me. Because I want you to know that of course Mamma and I will see to it that all your expenses here . . ."

Terence thanked him but told him that the press-agent had got there first.

"And then I want to thank you."

"*Thank* me?"

"From the bottom of my heart. Everything's so marvelous. . . ."

"Good heavens,—is it?"

"Everything except what's happened to you, of course, sir."

"Thanks—the wound's not serious, fortunately."

"Oh, I don't mean your wound, sir. I mean this little item." He pointed to the brief paragraph about indictment in the newspaper. "Is there anything I could do for you, sir?" he asked. "I'm in a bit of a rush now— Mamma and I are catching a plane in a few hours and there's still a lot to do—but if we could fix up some kind of a statement out West and mail it back, swearing that you spent that evening with us . . ."

Terence said he was afraid that wouldn't work.

"I'll gladly do anything you can think of, sir. I'll never forget I owe everything to you." And when Terence asked him just what he meant he opened the *Times* again, this time to the notice of the opening-night, and told him of Iris's exit and the Hollywood sequel. "Now I have to be going," he said. "My mother asked me to be sure to give you her greetings. She's as grateful to you as I am."

"*Grateful!* Good heavens! I see, though. . . . Well, good luck, Sanmartin."

"I've had plenty of that lately, sir, if I don't sound too callous toward you in saying so. Your being there to stop the bullet was the most marvelous luck. You see Mama and I would be happy today even if it was Iris that had stopped the bullet as Father intended her to before he caught sight of you. I mean—Father would be where he is no matter *who* stopped it. But we wouldn't be *as* happy as we are because with Iris shot I probably couldn't have made my debut. So you see how perfectly everything worked out. . . ."

That was all young Sanmartin had to say, except that when Terence inquired why his father was being sent to prison rather than to a psychiatric ward or an insane asylum, the boy answered, "The lawyers say that's out, sir. They won't even put in an insanity plea—they know in advance it would be useless. No jury would believe that anybody who's made as much money as my father is crazy."

And Terence barely had time, after Jack left, to read, with feelings of pride and concern that surprised him, the drama critic's and night-club editor's remarks on

Myra, when his door was pushed open again. "Terry, my sweet!"

"Iris! Well, this *is* . . ."

"Don't say you're surprised, dear lamb. Just tell me you're glad I'm happy again." Beautiful in her sables, decked with orchids, and spreading fumes of perfume and gin, she advanced to the bed and kissed him on the forehead, making tender sounds. "Here's Penn to see you," she said. "You're the first. We haven't seen another soul."

A blonde young man followed Iris into the room, propelling himself in a wheel chair, and he and Terence shook hands. He too had a ginnish aroma.

"You must become dear friends," Iris said. "You're dear friends already. We're *all* dear friends. . . . Penn's so sweet, Terry. So tender-hearted. Do you know why he came back to me? Because you disappointed me so horribly. When his family told him that the man I was seeing turned out to be a killer, Penn didn't turn more against me as they thought he would—he got terribly worried about my safety. He was upset about how upset I must be, and couldn't stay away another minute. And then—do you know what made him realize he was still passionately in love with me? Seeing me with you in the opera bar. When he saw my loyal nature—saw that despite all the scandal I was still loyal to you, and was even willing to appear with you in public—he knew he still loved me madly."

"You mean the night at the opera, when you slapped . . . ?"

"Now, Terry—don't hold a grudge. Penn started to come over toward me through the crowd, but then there was the shot and the stampede and he got knocked down, poor darling, and a little broken up again, but he'll soon be good as new. He got carted off to a hospital and didn't get out till last night. Oh, Terry—we're so happy, and we owe it all to you. . . ."

There seemed little use in trying to correct Iris about any part of all that.

"We've just dropped in here for a minute on our way to the preliminaries," she went on. "There has to be another ceremony, and that means those dreadful preliminaries again. We had so many martinis for breakfast Penn says he wants a Turkish bath before the preliminaries, so that's where we're actually going now. Please come and see us. In the family mansion, I mean—not the Turkish bath. Tee hee!"

They started to go. "Oh, I almost forgot. I was talking with Cynthia and Liz on the phone and they said something about your being in real trouble. Something in the paper this morning. Is anything wrong, Terry? Can we do anything to show our gratitude?"

"No, no," said Terence, politely. "Don't have me on your mind. Go out and enjoy yourselves. Just try to remember one thing, if you can. I'm not really a killer, you know. The criminal's probably a red-headed Irishman."

"You're not a killer? What do you mean? But it's because you *are* a killer that Penn came back!" Iris seemed upset, gave Terence a hostile look and Penn a worried one, and hurriedly wheeled Penn out, calling scarcely a farewell.

And then later in the afternoon Terence's door opened once more and although he had never before seen this visitor there was no doubt as to his identity: a ruddy-faced, cheerful-looking, husky young priest who wasted no time on preliminaries, but bluntly and energetically plunged into a matter that was troubling him. "Cousin Terence? Hello—I'm Vinny. Listen, I had no idea of this spot you're in. Aunt Kitty told me you'd been shot, and that your wound wasn't dangerous. But coming back on the Statue of Liberty boat I picked up a morning paper, and gosh . . . Doesn't Aunt Kitty know?"

"She'll find out eventually."

"Gosh, I hope somebody's *doing* something."

Smiling to himself at the oddity of this first conversation with a cousin, Terence told him of his case and explained where, rightly or wrongly, he felt his hope lay. "I have the idea," he said, "that if I could present my friend Ramsay with a solution of the mousetrap mystery, or with facts that would send *him* to a solution of it, he'd be too well disposed to me to hold back any longer, either consciously or unconsciously, whichever it is he's now doing, the fact that forms my alibi. So that's what I'm working on; that explains all these books."

Vinny frowned at the thought of the mousetrap intricacies. "Gosh, Terence, I wish I'd been more of a greasy grind at the seminary. If I had, maybe I'd be able to help you now. But Lord—I didn't even know Joseph was supposed to be dead by the time of the Crucifixion. I thought he was at the scene. I thought he was the one that wrapped the body in linen and put it in the tomb and rolled a rock in front. Where did I get all that from? Out of the air?"

Terence told him gently that he was almost correct but not quite: that he was confusing St. Joseph with the other Joseph—Joseph of Arimathea, the "good man and just" who had charged himself with Christ's entombment.

Vinny made a gesture of impatience with himself. "They used to warn us at the seminary not to get those two guys mixed up," he said. "But I guess I have more reason to mix them up even than most people. You see, I was stationed at Glastonbury for a while when I was in England with my outfit, and . . ."

"Your outfit?" Terence interrupted. "But you couldn't have been a chaplain—Aunt Kitty said you were just ordained a while ago. And seminary students were exempt from military service. So how come you were with an outfit?"

"Oh, some of us at the seminary were 'given a chance' to join up," Vinny said, emphasizing the phrase with a grin. "You know—some of us who'd been playing on the teams for years but never did much else around the place. I guess maybe they hoped enemy action would relieve them of having to decide what to do with us. They looked kinda desperate when we all turned up again wearing medals and everything and just as dumb as ever. Finally they decided to let us all be ordained anyway—just to get us out of the way. So now you know how I got to be a priest, Terence: I'm the dope of the family, I guess."

"If you are," said Terence, "you're dope number two, number one being yours truly. But what was that about Glastonbury?" And then he suddenly remembered something: "The Glastonbury Thorn!" he exclaimed. "I haven't thought of it in years. The Glastonbury Thorn! What is it, exactly? I used to know. It does have something to do with Joseph, doesn't it?"

"You're bloody right," said Vinny, blushing rather deeply as the expression, doubtless acquired in the outfit, emerged from a few inches above his clerical collar. "I mean, it certainly does. Joseph stuck it in the ground and it took root and it's still there. St. Joseph's quite a celebrity in Glastonbury. People talk about him all the time. That's why I got the two Josephs mixed up—I guess anybody who's ever been in Glastonbury thinks there's only one Joseph—only one St. Joseph, I mean."

Vinny's hopeless floundering in the rather simple matter of the two Josephs made it easy for Terence to imagine the desperation of his seminary teachers at his return from the wars, and it seemed kinder to change the subject. "Anyway, don't worry about me," he said, with somewhat more cheerfulness than he actually felt. "If the worst comes to the worst I'll be indicted for murder and fired from the university and tried. Somehow —maybe it's just my optimistic nature—I can't believe they'll ever really put me in the house."

"The house?" And as the meaning of the phrase dawned on Vinny the young man instantly looked stricken, lost his ruddy color, fell to his knees, leaned his forehead against Terence's bed sheet and burst into low-voiced prayer. His good heart and his concern and sincerity were so apparent that Terence felt an unfamiliar on-surge of cousinly affection. "Come now, Vinny," he said. "Get up and stop worrying. I shouldn't have said what I did: once I get things going everything will be all right. It's mean of me to spoil your trip to New York. What have you planned for tonight?"

"A real Chinese dinner and a tour of the Bowery," Vinny said, getting to his feet; and the reminder of the exotic pleasures to come was a quick banisher of gloomier thoughts. "I think I'll go home now and say hello to Aunt Kitty and maybe get her to give me a cup of tea, and then my buddies and I will wend our way Bowery-wards. We just saw it briefly from the sightseeing bus this morning and it sure packed a hell of a wallop. We agreed it was well worth a second visit. We all thought it was the most picturesque place we'd ever seen."

Terence agreed that the Bowery was picturesque. "But was it more so than things you saw in England?" he asked.

"Oh, *England!*" said Vinny, with a laugh that was clearly one of dismissal: a laugh that Terence had more than once heard in his army days, a laugh that was an expression of complete refusal to consider worthy of any judgment of any kind any place so odd as to be outside the U.S.A. And then Vinny left, promising to return the next day to see if he could be of help, and Terence lay in bed pondering. He gradually recalled the legend: that after the Resurrection Joseph of Arimathea had in some way got to Britain, planted a thorn staff which flowered, and on the site built the first British Christian church, since known as Glastonbury Abbey. But what, if anything, could Joseph of Arimathea and the Glastonbury Thorn have to do with *Saint* Joseph and the missing mousetrap?

CHAPTER ELEVEN

Sitting in her kitchen drinking tea with Vinny, Miss Quinn heard her front doorbell ring; and then, just about to rise to answer it, she heard a second, fainter sound—one that made her go all weak in the knees: she heard her front door-knob turn. Somebody, somebody unfamiliar with the fact that Manhattan house-doors are always kept locked, was doing what he had always done in Yonkers: after ringing, he was walking in, or rather trying to. "Vinny," said Miss Quinn, in a voice that she scarcely recognized as her own, "will you be a good boy and see who that is?" And as her nephew went briskly toward the door Miss Quinn lay back in her chair with her hand on her heart, trying to regain the self-control that the little sound had so instantaneously shattered. Breathing hard, trembling, she heard the door open, she heard voices, and then she heard the door close, and Vinny came back into the kitchen, alone. "Mistake," he said. "Fellow got the address wrong or something."

False alarm! Miss Quinn's heart sank and began to pound less, and for a moment everything seemed as before; but then suddenly she gave a great shriek that brought Vinny jumping to his feet in a panic. "Vinny! Vinny! What did he look like?" And when Vinny, in a few alarmed words, described the bell-ringer's appearance, Miss Quinn shrieked wildly again, rushed to her front door, flung it open, and stood on her stoop, crying "Gus! Gus!" at the top of her voice. Passers-by stared, but fortunately there were few of them, and down the block she spied him—not running, exactly, but going pretty fast—and she rushed down the steps and after him. "Gus! Gus!" Tears ran down her face; she was furious at herself for her headlessness: she *deserved* to lose him again, didn't she, allowing a man who was allergic to religion to be greeted at her door, after so many years, by *Vinny?* "Gus! Gus!" Near the corner of Sixth Avenue there were more people, and it was probably their staring that abashed him and made him stop. He stood there, facing her and looking scornful: the look he gave her almost broke her heart, but she knew she deserved it. Despite it, she threw her arms around him. "Only my nephew, Gus! Only a visitor! Nothing to do with us! He'll go to a hotel the minute I tell him to. Gus! What I said in the *Gazette* is true, every word of it: everything shall be as you so desire, Gus—everything . . . !"

CHAPTER TWELVE

Terence stayed awake much of the night, reflecting on Vinny's confusion. Confusion induced by thought was clearly of frequent occurrence in that pleasant young man's mind—as frequent, at least, as the presence there of thought itself. But it was his specifically *Joseph* confusion that interested Terence: it had been so instantaneous, so complete. And particularly interesting was the fact that this Joseph-confusion seemed to exist, or to have existed, elsewhere as well. According to Vinny —and Terence felt his cousin could be believed—an entire English town was confused about the Josephs, dazzled by the eminence of the more specifically local holy Joseph into confusing him with the elsewhere more celebrated saint. Furthermore, at the seminary Vinny had been warned "not to get those two guys mixed up." And there had certainly been confusion in someone's mind somewhere when a Joseph symbol as important as the mousetrap had been omitted from the supplementary panel of the triptych. Clearly, confusion about the Josephs was not uncommon.

Was this confusion of any value? Of any *practical* value, that is—value in relation to the remorselessly approaching indictment? There was a way of possibly finding out; and when breakfast had come and gone, and when the hospital doctor had made his daily examination of his shoulder, pronouncing it improved but in need of continued immobility, and firmly and not unexpectedly refusing the patient's request to be allowed to "do some errands downtown," Terence grimly took up the telephone and put in a call to Ramsay. Would he succeed in re-opening the subject of the mousetrap mystery, Ramsay having declared it closed and being, probably, ready to be testy if disobeyed? He was determined to try.

"Oh, Terence! How attentive! You want news of my health, no doubt? I think it must be better, whatever was wrong with it. I think they must be planning to send me home. They're testing my spinal fluid or something this morning, at any rate, and I can't imagine why they should do that if they were planning to keep me here: what difference does the composition of your spinal fluid make if you live in a hospital? It's only when you're out in polite society that your fluids have to be *sans peur et sans reproche*. By the way, Terence, speaking of laboratory tests, did you know that during the mouse mating season mouse urine is dangerous to humans? That's another charming detail I found in the *Handwörterbuch des deutschen Aberglaubens*. So— watch out! Also I forgot to tell you that not only mouse droppings, but mouse hearts, are aphrodisiac. Of course the hearts have to be powdered for the purpose. Maybe minced would be a better word. Minced mouse-hearts. Ugh! Thank goodness I've abandoned *that* mystery. But how are you, Terence? And what have you got to say for yourself?"

Terence took a deep breath. "Yes, I guess we are well out of that mystery, Ramsay. It was leading to such ridiculous theories. Imagine, I consulted a learned doctor of the church about it yesterday—purely for your sake, of course—and he told me that in his opinion the supplementary panel, where the mousetrap is missing, was probably added to the triptych in a part of the world where St. Joseph and his attributes aren't known, or where they're incorrectly known. What do you think of that?"

Ramsay laughed. "I'd think nothing of it, if I thought anything of it—I mean, if I thought about it at all, *if* you get what I mean. But I'm not thinking of it, as I told you I wouldn't. I've put it out of my head. It's a closed book. Besides, your learned doctor of the Church is presumptuous, to put it mildly. They've only had that triptych at the museum a couple of weeks, but don't you think I looked at the back of it as well as the front? It's all good Flemish oak, every bit of it, and all from the same boards, the supplementary panel as well as the rest. So . . . *Good-bye, Terence.*"

Ramsay's abrupt farewell, coming without warning through the receiver in a peculiar, piercing kind of whisper, took Terence by surprise; and the sudden clatter of Ramsay's instrument as he broke the connection almost did damage to his eardrum. Alarmed, Terence called back at once. For a long time he heard Ramsay's telephone ring without answer, and then came the breathless voice of a nurse. "Hello?" he said. "I just called back to see if Mr. Ramsay's all right. I was talking with him, and he hung up so suddenly that I wondered . . ."

"We're wondering too," the nurse said, panting. "We're wondering where he is. He was here a little while ago, but just now we heard his telephone ringing and ringing and we came in and found his room empty. People don't usually escape from here, but it seems that our outer door *was* unguarded for a minute or two just now, so heaven knows . . ."

She hung up, clearly distracted, and Terence shook his head. Ramsay's path was obviously the path that led from bad to worse, and the fact that "worse" in this case included his own now all but inevitable indictment did nothing to lessen Terence's depression over the fate of his friend.

But depression, at the moment, was scarcely sufficient, and a project partially conceived during the night now rapidly took shape, stimulated by the nurse's words: certainly he could temporarily absent himself from his hospital if Ramsay could escape from *his* institution! But attempts to dress, his one arm being strapped to his body, quickly proved fruitless; help was necessary, and he telephoned again. Once again he heard the other telephone ring and ring, and at long last came a drowsy voice. "Hello?"

"Hello? Aunt Kitty? You sound as though I woke you up."

"Yes, you did. Hello? Who is it?"

Terence glanced at his watch: after ten, and his aunt, who rose with the sun, was still abed and drowsy-voiced? "Aunt Kitty! What's wrong? Are you sick?"

A giggle came over the wire. "No, dear boy. Not sick at all. Just sleepy, dear. And happy. So happy. . . ."

Terence frowned: there seemed, in addition to his aunt's drowsy voice, to be a deep, a masculine mumble near her telephone.

"Terence darling, Gus sends you his best. Did you hear me? Gus sends you his best."

"Yes, I heard you, and . . . uh . . ." What was the right thing to say, under such circumstances, if by sternly suppressing all amazement and conjecture one concentrated on quickly finding it? Did one say "Congratulations"? No—one never congratulated the bride; just the groom. "Uh . . . Congratulate Gus for me, Auntie, will you? And to you I wish—what do I wish? Just all the happiness in the world, Auntie, and then more besides."

"How sweet you are, Terence! Thank you, darling.

You're my sweet nephew again, just like always. We'll see you soon, won't we? You'll come see us soon?"

"Of course I'll see you soon, Auntie." But not as soon as he had expected to: even with an indictment looming one doesn't disturb a bride by asking her to hurry to a hospital and help one dress. "Tell me, Auntie, is Vinny there?"

"No, dear, I'm sure he isn't. He told me he'd be setting out early today with his pals. Coney Island, I think —imagine, in this weather! I told him I wouldn't be a bit hurt if he spent last night in a hotel, but he said he didn't mind staying here at all, and Gus didn't mind having him when I explained he wasn't here in any religious capacity, so he stayed. What will his mother say! And his pastor!" Miss Quinn giggled again.

"They won't say anything if he doesn't, and probably he won't. Tell me, Auntie—have you Myra's telephone number?"

"*Myra's!* Why Terence . . . !" But apparently Miss Quinn—or rather Mrs. Lefferts—realized that it was her turn to be discreet, and she gave him the number without comment and they said farewell.

Terence hesitated before making his next call, and his voice was unsteady as he answered Myra's "Hello?"

"Myra—it's me."

"Oh . . . Are you better? Your arm, I mean?"

"Much better. But you? The paper said you looked badly. Have you rested?"

"Oh, I'm fine. But . . . Terence, what's going to happen to you? Can you really straighten things out? There must be *somebody* that saw you that night. . . ."

"Maybe there was. Maybe you could help me. If I dared ask for your help. You could help me by forgiving me, first. Could you do that?"

"I might."

"You wouldn't be sorry—at least I hope you wouldn't be. And then if you forgave me, maybe you could come over here. Now, I mean. Right now. Could you?"

"I might, especially if you told me one thing."

"What's that?"

"Nothing complicated—just . . . Oh Terence, just tell me—where are you?"

The hardest thing about sneaking out of a hospital is avoiding your own nurses and the other nurses and employees on your floor: once past them, you're among strangers, and safety is almost assured. "Why Professor Kelly! You're *dressed!*" one nurse exclaimed, coming upon Myra and Terence just as they were breathing with relief at gaining the shelter of a staircase. "Oh, I just slipped on a shirt and a pair of pants to see my fiancée part way out," Terence boldly answered. "Go away and let me kiss her good-bye."

"Kiss her good-bye and then get right back into bed," the nurse said severely. "I'll be in your room in two minutes and I want to see you in bed there when I arrive."

But in two minutes they were climbing into a taxi, and Terence was giving the address rather excitedly—not only because of the emotion of the get-away but because a thought had come to him: the thought that Ramsay had perhaps escaped from his nurses for the very reason that he was escaping from his, and that if that was the case perhaps Ramsay was at his destination already. If so, there was no time to lose: he wanted to be on hand if Ramsay was at work. "To the Art Museum and make it fast," Terence ordered. And as they grazed other cars in the mid-town traffic he and Myra did what they both full-heartedly realized they should never have stopped doing: they held hands and asked about each other. Terence described the intricacies of his own situation: "So remember," he said as they climbed the museum steps, "any reference he may let drop about my being with him that Wednesday evening. . . ."

Up in the elevator, through the sculpture gallery, into the painting rooms—Italian, French, Spanish, Flemish; a group of men in front of a picture; a loud voice—Ramsay's. He seemed barely to notice the arrival of Terence and Myra, so intently was he scolding the group of museum officials who stood before him. He had apparently been scolding them for some time, for they looked uncomfortable. "Since when am I not sent a copy of your record of a painting examination?" he was demanding, addressing them as a teacher would admonish a guilty class. "You're quick enough to get me down here and ask my opinion of a painting whenever you want it; I'm always glad to give it, and up to now you've always had the elementary courtesy to send me a copy of the technical laboratory findings. Why make an exception of *this* picture? Why? What's the reason?"

"But Mr. Ramsay," said one of them, braver than the rest but not quite brave enough, "we'd heard about your illness, and knew you were in a . . ."

"In a what, if you please? Where was I, exactly, that you felt privileged so grossly to neglect all politeness?"

"Why, in an . . ."

"In a hospital, Mr. Ramsay," said another, cravenly, and Ramsay treated him with the scorn he deserved. "Exactly. In a hospital, having a few of my fluids tested. So what? Even with fluids being tested I could still read, couldn't I? Read the most surprising painting examination record in years—findings that prove even *I* was fooled? When you've been looking at paintings as many years as I have, gentlemen, the discovery that you've been wrong is the greatest thrill that you can get; and to think that you should deprive me of it! So unkind, gentlemen! So ungenerous!" As Terence and Myra watched and listened, Ramsay's voice broke; he took a handkerchief and dabbed at his eyes. "You turn against me after years, gentlemen," he said, half sobbing. "A sorry way to requite a scholar's services of a lifetime!"

Was it a deliberately contrived act? Terence hoped so; he half expected Ramsay to give him a surreptitious glance or wink that would tell him it was—especially since the museum officials, themselves uneasy as to the exact nature of what was taking place, kept staring in embarrassment at the floor. But Ramsay gave no wink. Now he abruptly ignored the museum people. "Look, Terence. Look at that supplementary panel—the death of Joseph. So skillful! Such skillful repairs and repainting that even I was taken in. I! Imagine! I knew the wood was the same as that of the other panels, and I hadn't dreamed that the painting was different: it's so amazingly similar that no doubt had occured to me. I was so completely without suspicion that until today I hadn't even remembered that I hadn't seen the museum's x-ray report of the picture. They make one for every picture they acquire, you know, and I always get a copy. *most* unscientific of me to proceed even as far as I did, without a glance at it: when one begins to think one's self infallible, it's time to watch out. Of course I realize now that I should have been on my guard from the very beginning—from the moment I knew where the picture was found."

"Where was that, Ramsay?"

"But I *told* you it came from the West Indies, Terence. What's the matter with you? You used to pay attention, earlier in the course. I told you that Wednesday, that Wednesday night when you were so abominably rudely late for dinner."

The embarrassment of the museum officials, which had given signs of decreasing as Ramsay began his exposition, now became spectacular and pitiable as Terence, letting out a kind of war-whoop, gave Myra a passionate hug and then pointed at them as though in threat. "*What* night did Mr. Ramsay say?" he demanded. "*What* night?"

And one of them—the same yes-man who had said "hospital" to Ramsay—obligingly answered "Wednesday."

"Go ahead, Ramsay," said Terence, happily, his alibi secured. "Which West Indie did it come from? What's the story?"

And beaming at Myra and feeling himself a free man at last, he listened with somewhat less than full attention as Ramsay, after a few caustic remarks about bad classroom manners, told of how he had been misled by the fact the picture had been found in a chapel on the island of Maaba, a Dutch West Indie.

"It was your words of this morning, Terence, about 'a part of the world where St. Joseph and his attributes aren't known, or where they're improperly known,' that set me off," he said. "I rushed down here to the museum library and looked up Maaba in the encyclopaedia, and found that like so many of the West Indies it underwent a change of sovereignty a century or two ago: before being Dutch it had been British."

"British!" Terence almost laughed aloud: so his not-too-bright young cousin was, of all people, really turning out to be responsible for his alibi?

"Yes—British. That discovery gave me furiously to think. I had assumed that the picture had been brought directly to Maaba from Holland or Flanders; but now there was the probability that it had come via England. It was then that I thought of the x-ray report, and I rooted these charming gentlemen out of their comfortable offices and persuaded them to show me the report and the films—and sure enough, the supplementary panel showed signs of extensive repairs and repainting! *British* repairs and repainting: that was why I was fooled, of course—the British are as thorough in painting repairs as they are in everything else. 'Made in Britain' means something in art-restoring, you know, just as in boot-making and many another field. My theory is that the supplementary panel was damaged while being taken as loot by British troops in Flanders sometime during the seventeenth century wars, that it was repaired in England, and was then brought to Maaba by British colonists before the change in sovereignty. And underneath the repainting, Terence—underneath the repainting, in the original paint, the x-ray showed clear traces of—"

"The mousetrap!"

"The mousetrap. Of course. It was there all the time. It was the British restorers, who, unappreciative of its significance, probably even considering it a too homely, unworthy detail, had not included it in their repainting, thus fooling us all—fooling everybody except the x-ray. And this fact, Terence, the fact that the mousetrap was there originally but was not reproduced, that it was wilfully omitted, makes my 'detective story' about the triptych all the more fascinating: for it makes it possible for me to state, with almost complete certainty, that what might be called 'a confusion in Josephs' took place, and to determine in precisely which town in all of England the repainting was done!"

Ramsay looked so proud, so triumphant, so satisfied with himself, that Terence bit back the place-name that leapt to his lips. "I won't ask you the name of the town, Ramsay, eager as I am to learn it," he said. "I'm sure you'd rather keep it to yourself now, and reveal it only when your 'mystery' is published, wouldn't you?"

And Ramsay, expressing with a glance his recognition of Terence's delicacy, regarded the rest of the group assembled before him with the look signifying "Well, that's all for today," with which he had been wont to end his classes.

"And now," said Terence, "now we celebrate." And linking an arm through one of Ramsay's and motioning to Myra to do the same, he led them out of the gallery, hesitating only long enough to impress on his own mind the face of the museum official who had so obligingly echoed "Wednesday," in case his testimony should later be needed. "Good-bye, gentlemen," Ramsay called back to the museum people, who still stood huddled before their triptych, still bewildered, it seemed, at having been so suddenly convoked by someone they had thought confined behind bars, and so imperiously ordered to produce documents. One of them was still holding the x-ray record and films, not daring to take them back to the file, apparently, until the terrible Ramsay should have disappeared. "Good-bye," Ramsay called. "Remember to treat me less barbarously next semester." And in the highness of his spirits over the solution of his mousetrap mystery he did a series of little hops, skips and jumps, his arms linked in the arms of the others, as they left the gallery, gained the staircase and walked out of the building.

He was humming gaily as they got into a taxi, and when Terence, having given the address of headquarters to the driver in a low voice, said "Ramsay, I want you to tell just one more person I was with you that Wednesday." He cheerfully agreed. "Of course, dear boy. Of course. Anyone—anyone at all. How cold the canapés were by the time you arrived! Ugh! And you talked about Paris. . . ."

By rights, Terence reflected on the way downtown, two other people should be accompanying them: Vinny, whose Joseph-confusion had brought about the happy ending about to come, and Joe Giuliano, who would so relish the Inspector's admission that Terence was no longer a suspect.

At headquarters they were shown into the Inspector's office and the Inspector himself gave them his chilly stare across his desk. "Yes, Professor Kelly? I thought you were hospitalized. What is it?"

"It's simply that I have my alibi, Inspector. This is my fiancée, Miss Drysdale, and this is my friend Mr. Ramsay, who has something to tell you."

The Inspector started. "Ramsay?" he cried—much as Mr. Harwood, the public relations officer of the university, had cried a week or two before. "Did you say Ramsay?"

Terence nodded. "Be good enough to tell the Inspector, Ramsay, what evening it was I spent at your flat, will you?"

Ramsay told, quite simply and directly, that Terence had passed the Wednesday evening with him, and Myra confirmed, as a witness, that Ramsay had volunteered the information, without coercion or prompting, a short time before at the museum, and Terence said that if a fiancée's testimony wasn't good enough further confirmation could be obtained from one or more of the museum officials. "So," he said, "I guess that's that, Inspector. Am I free?"

The Inspector motioned to two of his assistants who were standing near. "Secure him," he said. "Strait jacket. Notify the institution." And almost before it was possible to realize what was happening, Ramsay had disappeared—without a struggle, without a sound. It was as though he had never been there. As he was hurried off he turned and gave Terence an odd little smile and shrug, as though to say, "The mystery's solved, isn't it? The mousetrap's found. So what do *I* care?"

For a moment there was silence—long enough for Terence to realize that although he was surprised by the suddenness of Ramsay's seizure, he was not, alas, surprised by the fact.

"Every precinct in New York and every police department out of town has been alerted about your friend Ramsay," the Inspector said, staring at Terence. "This morning, after final tests, just before he escaped, he was certified as hopelessly insane. How come you were traveling around with him, keeping him at large? You'll be lucky if you're not charged with endangering the public welfare. And whereas Mr. Ramsay's testimony might have been acceptable up until this morning, you don't think—you don't think, Professor Kelly, do you?—that we'll accept the word of a certified insanity case in support of an alibi for a murder? Good day, Professor Kelly. Try again."

The hospital's alarm for Terence reached headquarters a few minutes after he and Myra had left.

CHAPTER THIRTEEN

After an early, before-the-opera dinner at Liz's, Cesi and Zug kept Penn at the dining-table. It was time, they said, that he be brought up to date on at least the best of the stories that had been going the rounds while he'd been in Reno and Aiken. The Three took their coffee into the living-room. They weren't being prudish: they'd just heard all the stories a good many times already.

"I don't feel nearly so bitter toward Terence any more," Iris confided to the others as they sat by the fire. "As I told him yesterday in the hospital, it was really his turning out to be a killer that brought Penn back to me; and today, now that the ceremony's over, I wouldn't even mind if it turned out he really *wasn't* a killer, like he says he isn't."

The others agreed that there was no longer any reason to hold a grudge against Terence. "Shall I call him up and tell him we forgive him?" asked Liz. "Maybe they'd let him out of the hospital long enough to take in *Carmen*. Do you think he'd like to join us there?"

"I'm sure he'd like to join us anywhere," Cynthia said, and Liz telephoned the hospital, only to be quizzed with surprising rudeness, by someone who claimed to be a member of the hospital's administrative staff, about her "connections" with Professor Kelly, and finally, after her explanations, to be told a bit dryly that he "unfortunately wasn't available—not even for an opera invitation." The others shrugged when she reported the conversation. "Let's wash our hands of him, then," said Cynthia. "The latchstring's out if he wants to use it, but let's leave it up to him entirely."

When the men appeared, it turned out that not only stories but opera thoughts had been occupying them. "We've decided we're not going," Cesi announced. "It's in French, so *I'm* not going, and it's opera, so Zug's not going, and Penn—well, Penn's not going either, are you, Penn?"

Penn shook his head happily: how good it was to be

out of Aiken and one of the boys again with Cesi and Zug!

The Three accepted the decision with their habitual good nature. "But where the hell *can* we go, all dressed up like this?" Liz inquired.

As usual, Cynthia had an answer. "Remember the old rule," she said. "If you can't show off where everybody's dressed, then show off someplace where nobody's dressed."

"The Faculty Club!" said Iris, and everybody laughed as they had laughed several times before when she had described her lunch at the club with Terence, and the behavior of the professors and the looks of the lady faculty members.

"Exactly," said Cynthia. "Someplace dreary, that needs a touch of us. I was thinking of some run-down little bistro. . . ."

Vinny, arriving to take his last meal in New York with his aunt, was awfully apologetic about being the bearer of such bad news. "But I thought you ought to know the spot he's in," he said. "I didn't say anything to the hospital people, but I half thought I'd find him here. Where do you suppose he can be?"

"I can telephone Myra," quavered Mrs. Lefferts, explaining to Vinny and Gus who Myra was. "He asked me for her number. Maybe she knows." But Myra was not at home, and the Park-Yorkshire had no idea when she would be, for this was Wednesday, the one night of the week when Miss Drysdale did not perform in the Grizzly Bar. "You could get her at the theatre," the hotel operator suggested. "Her act begins at ten o'clock sharp."

Mrs. Lefferts thanked him and hung up and began to cry, and Gus patted her shoulder and told her to keep a stiff upper lip. "What time did you say your bus leaves?" he asked Vinny, politely successful in his attempt to banish from his voice any hint of his belief that as long as a priest was in the house disaster could only be expected to continue.

"Nine p.m.," said Vinny. "That gets us to Boston time enough for me to catch a train out home and wash up and report to the boss bright and early. Yep, my career begins tomorrow. It's been a swell visit to New York, Aunt Kitty. I wish I didn't have to leave just when everything's so upset."

"I hope you won't think of changing your plans on our account," said Gus, solicitously. "I have a feeling in my bones Terence will be all right tonight, Kitty, or tomorrow at the latest. After dinner we'll take Vinny to his bus and then go see this Myra at the theatre if it will make you feel easier. OK?"

His wife wiped her eyes, thanked him for being so good to her, and began to set her table.

"Well? Have we decided?" Joe Giuliano asked gaily as he arrived for his usual evening visit at the hospital. "Are we going to name him Terence if the professor gives us permission? Shall I go upstairs and ask him now?"

Sadie looked somber. "I don't imagine you'll find him interested at the moment," she said. And she showed him the item in the morning paper. Joe said a few crackling words about the Inspector, and that he'd go upstairs and see if there was anything he could do. He returned glum. "He shouldn't have done it," he said, after telling Sadie the news. "Running away's like an admission of guilt. I suppose he got panicky. I wish I knew his hide-out. I'd try to persuade him to come back. As it is . . ."

After they left headquarters Terence told the taxi driver to take them slowly up the East River Drive, and in low voices he and Myra discussed his plight. "To recapitulate," he said, "the alibi's gone. Vanished. You can't blame anybody: there's a point at which a lunatic's sane moments cease to be trustworthy. Lack of alibi means indictment. Indictment means that my resignation's put through. And no matter what happens in court, I don't have to tell you that a professor who's ousted in a murder scandal has a rough road ahead of him in academic life. But that's looking far ahead. What do we do *next*? Do I just give up and let myself be led to jail? The university lawyers won't touch me, and my own was worse than useless."

"Do you remember," asked Myra hesitantly, "that I sent down mine?"

Terence kissed her. "This time," he said, penitently, "I accept."

But Myra, after going into a telephone booth, returned to Terence in the waiting cab with the news that the attorney was out of town, expected back late in the evening. "I'll call him at his home," she said, "but there's no use doing it for several hours. Why don't we ride around a while, then have a bite in some quiet spot, you come to the theatre with me, stay in my dressing room, and when I'm through I'll phone him. Since you've got to spend a few more hours without counsel that seems to me the best way to spend them."

Terence agreed, and they drove slowly about in the park. There was, they discovered, a difference of opinion between them concerning a point of behavior: whether it would be perfectly honorable, or whether it would be despicable and caddish, for Terence to propose just now, when he was faced with so many disasters, including pauperism.

"If you want to know whether I'll marry you," said Myra, "as you indicate you do want to know, the thing to do is to ask me."

"But it would be low-down to ask you now," Terence protested. "At the moment, I'm a drowning man; I should be on my feet to propose."

"As you choose," said Myra, coolly—so coolly that Terence proposed at once.

"And our engagement dinner?" he asked, after being accepted. "I'd like it to be a gala affair. Whereas actually, considering that the hospital has probably announced my disappearance to the police, and that the police have probably got preparations for indictment well under way, your idea of 'a quiet spot' is probably good. A hole in the wall, I should think: an unlikely dump of some kind."

"Some place very near the hospital," Myra suggested. "They'd be less likely to think of looking for you there."

"Drive us around in the East Fifties," Terence told the driver. "We'll tell you when to stop."

Darkness had long since fallen, and as they were stopped by a traffic light on Second Avenue near Fifty-Ninth Street Terence caught sight of a neon sign and said "What about here? It seems as good as anyplace." And they got out and he paid the driver and they went in.

"Here's one with a sweet name," Cynthia cried, as the limousine cruised slowly as per instructions. "It looks right, somehow, don't you think? Let's try it."

All eyes were on them as they entered, The Three in their ermine, sable, mink, feathers and jewels, the men in top hats, and Penn, to make it a bit more picturesque, in his chair. "Oh, my God!" cried Myra; and Terence, surprised while drinking coffee, choked and coughed so loudly that all eyes turned on him instead. "It's Terry!" shrieked Iris. "And darling Drysdale!"

There was no avoiding the introductions, the changing of places, the putting together of tables, the general hilarity. And in response to the inevitable "What in the world are you doing *here?*" It seemed better to say not "Lying low while waiting for a lawyer," but rather the other part of the truth: "Celebrating our engagement."

"Engagement! *Dio mio!* Isn't this the *darlingest*, the most *unexpected* . . . ! Waiter—champagne! You're the nicest, the party-causingest *ragazzo, caro Terenzio!*"

The redhead was quiet tonight. A few at the bar, dinner in a booth, and now back at the bar again, peaceful as could be. He'd brought few balloons with him: he'd had a good selling day, evidently, and was treating himself with the proceeds. The bartender knew about what to expect, by now. Few balloons meant enough money for a meal, and pretty quiet behavior. Many balloons meant money for drinks only, and less quiet behavior. Furthermore, the redhead was evidently a nervous type, sensitive, and even on his quiet nights he reacted rather fast to any unusual activity around him, any disturbance. Like the recent night that had been one of his quietest until some souse without the sense to mind his own business had yelled in his ear: "Take ya gloves off, mug!" A free-for-all had resulted from that, and it had almost been necessary to call the police. Even a racket confined to other customers, quite unconnected with him, sometimes made him jittery. So that when the swells came in, and saw their friends, and started making a noise and throwing a party, the bartender looked at the redhead rather anxiously. But he kept on behaving, behaving perfectly.

Vinny's bus left from the new terminal near Bloomingdale's, and when they arrived there with him, and he'd introduced them to his friends, two young fellows dressed in black like himself, his Aunt Kitty declared that she felt too nervous and upset about Terence to want to sit around and say any prolonged farewells. "Take me away, Gus," she begged. "It's silly of me—I know Vinny's not going far, and I'm sure I'll see him again, but I just feel sentimental. Take me away before I begin to act foolish."

So good-byes were rather hasty, and Kitty made a gulping escape as Vinny called out last-minute repetitions of his thanks. "I'll pray for Terence," he cried, and Gus murmured to himself, as he hurried after Kitty, "Don't bother, padre. Just get on your bus, and Terence will take care of himself."

"It's too early to go to the theatre yet," he said, when they were out on the street. "Let's stop in along here for a beer, shall we? I like the looks of these places: they look friendly. I bet they serve pickles on the side."

Kitty nodded mutely, took his arm, and turned for a last look through a window of the bus station, where three black-clad young men could be seen sitting on a bench, laughing among themselves just as though at least one of them, such a sweet fellow, too, wasn't going back to live—and probably quite happily—among narrow-minded, bigoted people who wrote letters about their sisters to old ladies' homes. On the other hand, Kitty reflected, if her sister May *hadn't* written her disgusting letter, would she and Gus be on their way to beer and pickles now? And to go back one step further, if Terence hadn't stayed away from her on his birthday night, she wouldn't have written to Mount St. Margaret's in the first place. So it was really Terence, if you looked at it that way, who had got Gus back. . . .

"Terence!" screamed Mrs. Lefferts, preceding Gus to a table when they had turned into the place he thought the friendliest-looking of all. "Terence!"

Once again the bar-tender looked anxiously at the red-head as the table of swells incorporated, with a maximum of introductions and fuss, the two newcomers into their number. No—he wasn't quite as calm as he had been. He was staring at the table-full, frowning, and beginning to mumble to himself and to fidget. . . .

"Shall I stop in on the Inspector on my way home?" Joe asked. "Just to tell him what I think of him for persecuting a swell fellow like the Professor till he runs away and hides like a dog? I'd do it, for two cents."

Sadie said she wouldn't put up the money for that, but she urged him to do something else on the way home by all means. "I know you don't like to drink alone," she said, "but do stop in someplace and take a swallow medicinally. Please. It will relax you, and you won't stay awake all night brooding."

It was Gus who began everything.

He wasn't used to champagne. The least little bit of it went to his head and made him giggle. He didn't realize that, and had anybody suggested it he would have denied it indignantly. He could drink large quantities of other things without being affected, couldn't he? So he could. But champagne was different. What he *thought* was affecting him was the way these friends of Terence's were talking and acting—the way they all called everybody "Darling," the way all three of the men kept kissing all three of the women, the way one of the women kept declaiming—that was the only word for it —declaiming nonsense, such as: "The recent almost simultaneous appearance—somewhat unexpected, it must be admitted, considering the temper of the world about us, and all the more gratifying for that—of new translations of the *Aeneid* into Sardinian, Romansch and Provençal . . . Isn't that *perfect*, Terence? I haven't forgotten a word. Not a word. And the thesis is still waiting for you at the flat. When will you come for it, Terry dear? We don't need lessons any more, but do come soon, Terry, and bring this sweet dear Drysdale. . . ."

Gus felt such talk as that going inexplicably to his head. "Look at that redhead," he said, giggling. "That redhead at the bar. He's eating pickles with his gloves on. That's not the way to eat pickles. Spoils the flavor. Spoils the gloves. I'll tell him, for his own good."

He stood up, even though Kitty begged him not to. "*Please*, Gus," she whispered. "Please be quiet, sweetheart. Please."

"Now Kitty," he said, patting her hand. "Remember: 'Everything shall be as you so desire.' Remember?" He got up and moved toward the bar.

"And how is everybody at the club, Terry dear?" Iris was saying. "How's that sweet old Professor Hall, with his marbletop table and everything?"

Terence smiled, and was now for the first time able to tell Iris—discreetly not repeating all of Professor Hall's exact language—about the old gentleman's invitation. "I shan't be able to go with you," he said. "My time's going to be taken up. But I'm sure the professor and his wife would love to see you and Penn. Take along Cynthia and Liz and Cesi and Zug, too: it would be a Sabbatum the Halls would never forget."

With a laugh, Iris put the Halls out of her mind forever. "And the other cute old thing?" she chattered on. "How's he? The one you called Ramsay. The one we read about in the paper later."

"Ramsay? Did you meet Ramsay?"

Terence had forgotten it; and he was also imperfectly acquainted with Iris's steel-trap memory—a trait she shared with the others of The Three—for anything to do with a man, even Ramsay. "Certainly I met him," she said. "Don't you remember how cute he was? He didn't say a word to me. Didn't even seem to see me. Terribly cute. Just talked to you as if I wasn't there, about . . ."

"Talked about what?" Terence demanded, agitatedly. "About . . . ?"

But Liz was distracting everyone with sounds of delight. "Look, darlings! Balloons! How perfect!" And she was distributing balloons to all, taking them from a cluster she'd found in a corner of the bar and grille. "Balloons, children! The party's perfect! I haven't seen balloons since I was tiny, tiny, tiny. . . ."

"Yes you have, Liz," said Cynthia, in her raucous, night-cap voice. She sounded bossy, and even a little disagreeable, as though she perhaps thought people hadn't paid enough attention this evening to her thesis-reciting. "Yes you have. Just the other night you were talking about balloons."

"Not since I was tiny, tiny, tiny. . . ."

"Yes. Just the other night. You said the night of the murder you and Cesi drove past the hat shop and you saw . . ."

"No. Not since I was tiny, tiny, tiny. . . ."

"So what if you're a book-binder?" Gus was saying at the bar, so loudly and tipsily that Kitty hid her face in her hands. "*I'm* a pickle-salesman, and I'm telling you that to eat pickles with your gloves on . . . Being a book-binder doesn't affect the question. It wouldn't make any difference if you were a . . ." Gus looked around the room; multi-colored balloons were floating over the table he had left. ". . . a balloon-seller," he said. "Even if you were a balloon-seller, to eat pickles with . . ."

"I'm not a balloon-seller!" the redhead shouted, pounding his glass on the bar and lunging toward Gus. "I'm a book-binder, I tell you. A book-binder. . . ."

"*What* was Ramsay talking to me about that day at the club?" Terence asked Iris beseechingly.

But so much was going on, with Liz and Cynthia bickering, and Gus and the redhead shouting at each other, and now suddenly the tall figure of Joe Giuliano —where in the world had *he* come from?—coming in through the door and striding up to the redhead and loudly demanding: "You're a *what*, did I hear you say? A *what*? Say it again."

"A book-binder, that's what I am. . . ."

"A book-binder, are you, and red-headed, and even Irish-voiced. . . ." Joe was shouting louder than anybody.

"And think of him, eating pickles with his *gloves* on," cried Gus reproachfully. "*Pickles . . . !*"

"The night of the *murder*," Cynthia insisted to Liz. "The *murder*. Yes, you did. You said you and Cesi drove right past that hat shop after dropping Zugie and me, and on the street you saw somebody carrying balloons and something that looked like a bottle. . . ."

"Book-binder like ----!" Joe was shouting at the bar, and Terence was jumping up to rush over and help him, because quite a fight was developing and the bartender and the waiters were trying to separate the two, and Kitty had run over and was pulling Gus away. But Iris was talking. "Don't you remember how cute he was? How he didn't look at me at all, and just told you that in connection with what you and he had been talking about two nights before he'd been reading about mouse-traps? Don't you remember that? *I* do."

Terence gave a shout, and, just as a few hours before in the museum, he hugged Myra passionately. "Joe!" he cried. "Hold him! I'm coming!"

"Why, so I did, Cynthia," Liz admitted, remembering. "So I did. My God!" she screamed. "There's a balloon man *here! Murder! Murder!*"

And as Terence joined the fray at the bar, police whistles blew, the doors burst open and night-sticks began to fall.

"Don't you hit *me*, you blue-coated bastards," cried Joe. "There's your man, that redhead, and you can tell the Inspector I said so!"

CHAPTER FOURTEEN

It wasn't quite as simple as that, of course.

Joe did get knocked by the night-sticks—more than he might have hadn't he given the police so convincing an impression of being their chief antagonist. For a few moments they were so busy fighting Joe that the redhead almost escaped. But Terence and Gus each grabbed one of the redhead's legs, and Terence succeeded in giving the police some faint understanding of who was who. The Three and their husbands were allowed to ride to headquarters in Liz's limousine under police surveillance, and the others were driven in the van: Mrs. Lefferts, at Terence's request allowed to choose, loyally elected to share her friends and relatives' disgrace.

Nothing took very long, thanks to the anonymous letter. The moment the now sullen redhead signed the register it was clear that he was its author; and the Inspector ordered him held and everyone else freed— everyone except Terence. "Until this man's convicted there's still the formality of the alibi, Professor," he said. "So we'll just keep you, since we've got you here." But Iris, with her memory of what Ramsay had said at the Faculty Club, quickly took care of that, and Terence walked out of headquarters now definitely free, bound only, along with the others, to testify when the time came. "Vinny should really be here too," he said to his aunt after he'd thanked everyone and kissed her. "He came close to really helping me: it wasn't his fault that he didn't turn the trick." Gus smiled to himself: he was convinced that Vinny *had* turned the trick, simply by getting on his bus. But he knew there was no reason to tell the others so. Everyone crowded into the limousine, and the first stop was Myra's theatre—it was almost ten o'clock. "Good-bye, Terry darling!" The Three cried, and Cynthia reminded him once again of his thesis, awaiting him in her living-room whenever he wished to call. Then the Lefferts and Joe were dropped off, Mrs. Lefferts insisting that Joe come in for an arnica rub.

"Well," demanded Cesi, when the original party was again alone in the car, "aren't we all sorry we didn't go to the opera?"

Everyone sighed happily, especially Penn. "So much fun to be back with you all," he said, feelingly, squeezing Iris's hand.

"Bless that Terry," said Iris, and the others echoed her.

CHAPTER FIFTEEN

"It's so ridiculous and puzzling," said Terence. "The new program was obviously crazy—I'd never have inaugurated it if I hadn't been in some kind of a state. And yet, fiasco though it was, a lot of people have benefited from it in one way or another: my aunt, Iris, Jack Sanmartin and his mother, the Giulianos . . ."

"Yes, it is ridiculous and puzzling," said Myra. "But isn't everything, really?"

Reflecting, as she was, that she was with Terence at this very moment because of the chance publication in a newspaper of an account of his *amourette* with somebody else, Myra could perhaps be excused for saying so.

But Terence, on second thought, wasn't sure he fully agreed. "Well, it's certainly *puzzling*, the way things turn out well or badly without rhyme or reason," he said, his good arm around her, "but are you sure *ridiculous* is the right word?"

They were in Terence's room at the hospital, where Myra was paying her usual pre-theatre evening visit. "I had a call from Max today," she said. "He'd just heard from the record company. Poor Lily White! Her records aren't doing well at all. It's not that she's not talented— she is. But it seems all this publicity about me makes people think of Drysdale, not White, in connection with harpsichords. So I'm to do a set of records. They want to call it 'Blue Harpsichord.' Max was pretty excited. He kept saying 'Smashed potatoes!' for some reason. 'Smashed potatoes, Myra! You're a success story, from the cradle to the grave!'"

They were speaking of Ramsay—of what he might need, or accept, of his friends, wherever it was he'd be living—when there was a knock on the door and Joe Giuliano came in. "Well, tonight we're taking him home," he said. "He's fine and Sadie's fine and they need the room for somebody else. He can be your namesake, can't he? And you'll both come to the christening?"

And when he had a yes to both his questions Joe asked a third, a bit more hesitantly. "That thesis of yours," he said. "I heard one of those dames say she was keeping it till you called. I don't know how you'll feel about this, considering everything that's happened, but —wouldn't you like me to bind it for you?"

Terence hesitated a moment. Then he smiled. "I don't see why not," he said, tightening his good arm around Myra. "Even toward that thesis I haven't any hard feelings. Have you, darling?"

THE END